The Millionaire's Christmas Wish

SHAWNA DELACORTE

™SILHOUETTE
DESIRE®

First published in Great Britain 1999
Large Print edition 2001
Silhouette Books Limited,
Eton House, 18-24 Paradise Road,
Richmond, Surrey TW9 1SR

© SKDennison, Inc. 1998

ISBN 0 373 04711 8

Set in Times Roman 16½ on 17½ pt.
36-1201-55968

Printed and bound in Great Britain
by Antony Rowe Ltd, Chippenham, Wiltshire

SHAWNA DELACORTE

travels as often as time permits and is looking forward to visiting several new places during the forthcoming year while continuing to devote herself to writing full-time.

One

———

Marcie Roper shifted the weight of her packages and cradled them in her other arm as she stared at the slinky evening gown in the store window, each sequin shimmering an iridescent peacock blue. She allowed an audible sigh of resignation as she glanced down at her faded jeans. It was certainly a beautiful gown, but she would never go any place where such a dress would be appropriate. It was just not the type of life-style she had settled into. She sighed again as she moved along to the next window displaying a red silk cocktail dress. She noted that all the store windows were already decorated for the Christmas holiday season in spite of the fact that Thanksgiving was still a couple of weeks away. A moment of sadness touched her—even though she had friends, it would be another holiday season to be spent alone.

"Hey! Wait a minute!"

The shouted command grabbed her attention. She glanced down the street just in time to see a tall man—in his mid-thirties, she guessed—appear from around the corner. He headed in her direction at an easy, loping gait. His tanned good looks and athletic build were hard to ignore. She stepped closer to the building to clear a path for him.

As he ran toward her, he shrugged out of his red windbreaker, turned it inside out to a charcoal gray color and jammed his arms back in the sleeves. He stole a quick look over his shoulder, then pulled a baseball cap from his back pocket and covered his hair. He turned back toward her and for an instant their gazes locked. Then he came to an abrupt halt.

His sky-blue eyes twinkled with amusement. Her first thought had been that he was in some sort of trouble, but the mischievous grin that tugged at the corners of his mouth told a different story. He reminded her more of a little boy who was about to pull off a prank than of someone being chased by a person or persons unknown.

The tall stranger stared at her for a moment before once again glancing over his shoulder. Apparently satisfied that he was sufficiently ahead of his pursuer, he sidled up beside her and put his arm around her shoulder. He positioned himself so that he faced away from the corner, and extended an engaging smile. It was the type of smile that said, "Trust me," even though the devilish twinkle in his eyes said something quite different.

"I'd sure appreciate it if you could spare me just a minute or two of your time."

Chance Fowler tossed a furtive glance over his shoulder just as a short, balding man came huffing and puffing around the corner. The paunchy man had a camera bag slung over his shoulder, one camera suspended from a strap around his neck and another camera in his hand. There was no doubt in Chance's mind that the man was yet another tabloid photographer in search of candid shots of the heir apparent to the Fowler family fortune and Fowler Industries.

It usually annoyed him, especially if he was involved in one of his personal projects. His upbringing may have been one of wealth and privilege, but that did not make him immune to the plight of the disadvantaged. With his mother's encouragement he had decided as far back as college that he would give back to society in general what had been handed him simply as his birthright. As far as Chance was concerned, his efforts to provide disadvantaged older youth and high school dropouts with viable work skills and find opportunities for employment was no one's business but his and the people involved in his training school. He had no desire to put a spotlight on those activities or those he was trying to help.

But every now and then, when he did not have any pressing matters dictating his actions, he liked to make a game of evading the photographers. And today was one of those days.

"Let me go this instant!" Marcie shook off the mesmerizing sound of this stranger's smooth, dulcet tones and engaging smile. She struggled to escape the arm he had draped around her shoulder in the type of familiar manner that said they were longtime friends.

Chance pulled her closer to him and touched his fingertip to her lips to still her words. "Just as soon as this photographer goes away."

Marcie glanced toward the camera-laden man. Her initial surge of fear settled as she realized she was not in any physical danger from this stranger, but was quickly replaced by a flash of anger. ''I'll do no such thing! You let go of me immediately or I'll call for help.'' She began to struggle again while trying to maintain a hold on her packages.

The set of the photographer's jaw and his tight grip on his camera told Marcie of his determination to find his quarry. He looked across the street, into a side alley, then started down the sidewalk toward her and the handsome stranger who continued to hold her within the curve of his arm even though she still struggled to get free.

The stranger quickly enfolded her in a complete embrace. His words tickled across her ear, the hypnotic quality of his voice lulling her into a momentary state of submission. ''I was hoping we could just stand here and pretend to be window-shopping together without any fuss, but I guess we'll have to do it this way instead.'' Before Marcie could react, he covered her mouth with his.

The photographer hurried past them without even slowing down. Shockingly aware of the heated sensuality of this stranger's kiss—a kiss that literally took her breath away and left her weak in the knees—Marcie barely noticed the man as he rushed down the street. She was having trouble collecting her thoughts.

No one had ever kissed her like that before or totally swept her off her feet the way he just had. If it were not for the fact that he had been holding her, her legs surely would have buckled. She fought to gain control of the thousands of butterflies that flitted about inside her stomach and the increased palpitations of her heart.

As soon as the danger passed, Chance started to break off the kiss, but he allowed his lips to linger against hers a second longer before pulling back. He looked into the startled, uncertain eyes of the woman in front of him, holding her gaze trapped within his for what seemed like an eternity. He was not certain what he was seeing, but he knew in an instant that he liked it. He also knew that he wanted more of this tantalizing woman. His gaze drifted across her delicately beautiful features to the lush fullness of her slightly parted lips. He wanted to kiss her again. He wanted to continue to hold her.

He tried to swallow the lump that had lodged in his throat as soon as he had broken off the kiss. He wanted to kick himself for having done something so foolish as to have involved this delectable stranger in one of his little games. It had definitely been a rotten idea. It would have been better for everyone concerned if he had just let the photographer take his picture.

A flustered and embarrassed Marcie quickly stumbled backward a couple of steps. She ran her fingers through her short auburn hair in a nervous attempt to smooth it away from her face as she clutched her packages against her body with her other hand. Her legs still felt wobbly, but not so much so that she could not turn and run away from this very bizarre encounter and this incredibly tempting man.

And run she did, as hard and as fast as her legs would take her. It was almost as if her emotional existence depended on getting as far away from this man as quickly as possible.

"Hey! Wait a minute—"

Marcie dashed down the street, her shoes pounding hard against the pavement with each step. She heard him call after her, but she dared not stop. As soon as she rounded the corner she ducked into a large store. Without pausing to look back, she walked swiftly through the store and out the other side to another street. Only then did she stop and glance back over her shoulder.

As soon as she was convinced that he had not followed her, she leaned back against the building to catch her breath. She juggled her packages, being careful not to spill the contents of one sack that had ripped open.

"Oh, damn!" The words came out loud and clear, her irritation audible for anyone within earshot. Somewhere during her flight from that absurd encounter with that very disconcerting stranger she had lost one of her packages—the one from the bookstore. It contained a special order she had placed two weeks ago. Three of the books were hers, but the fourth was a large volume about the Civil War that she had ordered as a birthday present for her father.

And now it was lost before she could even get it to the post office. She clenched her jaw in anger. It was all *his* fault. She had been minding her own business, doing a little window-shopping while making her way back to her car, when *he* had accosted her.

It had all happened so quickly. She had not

even gotten a good look at him—about an inch taller than six feet, dark blond hair with sun-bleached streaks that really set off his golden tan, sky-blue eyes with just a hint of wrinkling at the corners, handsomely chiseled features with a small scar on his chin, and an absolutely devastating smile. No, she certainly had not paid any attention to his physical presence and overwhelming appeal—not much she hadn't.

She cleared her throat, glanced around as if to make sure no one had eavesdropped on her totally inappropriate thoughts, then took a calming breath to ease her embarrassment. A little chill shivered across her nape. She immediately stilled it with her hand. She took another deep breath, held it for several seconds, then slowly expelled it as she shook her head.

It had certainly been a weird day. It had started out with a flat tire before she'd even left home to drive down to San Diego. She had done her shopping, been pulled into a totally off-the-wall encounter with a disconcerting stranger, then had lost a package containing four books.

And now it was time to go home.

She reclaimed her car, then drove north out

of San Diego to the mostly upscale bedroom community of Crestview Bay. She had a one o'clock meeting with a prospective client. A ripple of irritation passed through her body. Thanks to *him* she would have to skip lunch if she was going to be on time for her appointment.

Much to her chagrin the heated desire produced by his kiss still lingered in her consciousness. Irritably, she tried to shove it aside, but she was not able to totally eradicate the memory.

Chance Fowler pulled into the parking lot of the yacht club, parked his Porsche in his usual space, and hurried toward the sleek sailboat that bore the name *Celeste* in black letters on a gleaming white background. He had named the racing sloop after his mother—the first of what had turned out to be many women who subsequently claimed the name of Mrs. Douglas Fowler.

"How's it going, Take-A-Chance?" The shapely blonde in the hot-pink thong bikini waved from the deck of the boat two slips over from his. "Are you entered in the regatta tomorrow?"

"Sure am, sweetheart." Take-A-Chance…it was a label that one of his classmates had given him during college and it had stuck, even after all these years. Chance Fowler— always ready to take a chance on a new adventure, a new thrill, or a dangerous stunt.

"Then we'll see you at the party at the clubhouse afterward?"

"I expect so." He returned her wave, inconspicuously giving an appreciative once-over to her blatantly displayed charms. He thought the temperature was a little too cool for her to be dressed so skimpily, but that was Bambi. She was never one to keep her attributes under wraps.

"It's about time you got here!" The angry male voice came from the deck of the *Celeste*.

Chance boarded the sloop. "Sorry, Dave. I got held up avoiding another one of those damned tabloid photographers." Then, in response to the image of startled hazel eyes surrounded by long dark lashes, he added, "Although it might have been better if I'd just let him snap his picture—it certainly would have been quicker."

His brow furrowed in momentary concentration as he recalled for at least the tenth time in the past couple of hours exactly how the mystery woman had felt in his arms and the taste of her mouth. And there had been something in her eyes, something he could not quite place. Had it been a spark of passion? A heated moment of desire? Whatever it was had flickered through her eyes and disappeared before he could accurately read it. He wanted another opportunity to ignite that spark, but she had run off before he'd been able to discover who she was or where to find her. By the time he had gotten to the corner, she was nowhere in sight.

He closed his eyes and visualized her delicate features. When he had stared into her eyes, he'd been captivated by tiny golden flecks that sparkled brighter than the light glinting off the water in Mission Bay on a bright sunny day. Her lips were full and lush, her mouth—

"Earth to Chance…" Dave's irritation broke into Chance's momentary lapse of attention.

"Huh? Oh…sorry. I have several things on my mind."

"I don't have all day. Do you suppose you

could narrow that list down to just one item—like maybe tomorrow's regatta?''

''Yeah.'' Chance extended an apologetic smile. ''Sure thing.''

''Then let's get under way. Bonnie's sister, her husband, and their three kids are coming over for dinner tonight and I'm going to catch hell if I'm late again.''

Chance could not stop the laugh prompted by Dave's complaint. ''Bonnie's a lovely lady, but you're the one who was dead set on getting married. I tried to warn you about the pitfalls of marriage, but you refused to listen to me.''

Dave glared at his friend. ''Give it a rest, will ya?''

The two men quickly got down to the business of preparing for the next day's regatta and were soon under way as they passed from the yacht club basin out to open water.

Four hours later they returned to Chance's slip at the yacht club. After securing the sloop, Dave hurried toward his car. Chance watched his buddy pull out of the parking lot and head down the street before turning toward his own car. He was not in any hurry. It was Friday night, but he had no place special to go and nothing special to do. He had no desire to hang around the yacht club and socialize with a bunch of people he did not care that much about.

He looked at the package on the passenger seat of his car. The mystery woman had dropped it when she'd run off. He had picked it up, intent on following her to return it, but had lost sight of her when she'd disappeared around the corner. He had stuck the package in his car, with plans to do something about it later.

It seemed that *later* had finally arrived.

The outside of the sack bore the name of a downtown bookstore located just a block from where he had perpetrated his little charade. He opened the sack, hoping to find something inside that would tell him who she was. He removed four books and set them on the car seat, then reached into the bag again and withdrew a hand-written special order sales receipt. *Marcie Roper. Crestview Bay Nursery.*

He folded the sales slip and stuck it in his jacket pocket. A grin tugged at the corners of his mouth, leaving him a little uncertain about where it had come from or why. His breathing increased slightly and a tightness pulled across his chest accompanied by a soft warmth that settled over him. "Well, Marcie Roper...I've never had a woman literally turn and run from me before. I guess I'm going to have to see what I can do to change your apparent opinion of me."

He furrowed his brow in contemplation. He had never had an impromptu kiss grab him like that, either. He could still feel the heat of the moment and the desire that had flooded his consciousness as the enticing interlude played through his mind.

He returned his attention to the package she had dropped. He took a look at the books she had purchased. The special-order item was a large and expensive volume on the Civil War. In addition, there was the latest bestseller thriller, a biography of Catherine the Great of Russia, and a romance novel.

He put the books back in the sack, got out of his car and made his way to the yacht club office. Checking the phone books, he quickly grabbed the appropriate one, and flipped through the Yellow Pages until he found what he was looking for. He pulled the bookstore receipt from his pocket and jotted three names on the back of it. Crestview Bay Florist. Crestview Bay Nursery. Crestview Bay Landscaping. All three businesses had the same address. Then he looked in the white pages and found a listing in Crestview Bay for an M. J. Roper.

The image of her delicate features played across his mind—her kiss-swollen lips, the golden flecks in her hazel eyes. He shook his head as he walked back to his car. The entire incident had been nothing more than a fluke— a random encounter, a spontaneous moment. So why was it still so vividly real in his mind? Why could he still taste the kiss and feel her in his arms?

"Marcie Roper of Crestview Bay..." He stared at the sales receipt as he uttered the words. "You may have managed to slip away from me today, but it won't be quite so easy the next time we meet now that I know where to find you."

Marcie leafed through the Sunday newspaper while enjoying her morning coffee. It seemed that all the ads featured Christmas items even though the holiday was still almost six weeks away. It was difficult to think in terms of Christmas when the normal San Diego weather was so pleasantly warm and sunny that time of year.

She knew she needed to get busy setting up her displays for the limited number of Christmas items she carried at the nursery—a special line of handmade ornaments, indoor and outdoor wreaths, holly plants and cuttings, evergreen garland, poinsettia plants and Christmas trees. She found the holidays to be a lonely time and so far the spirit of the season had eluded her.

That was the way it had been for the past few years, since the death of her grandmother. In all her thirty-one years, it was her grandmother who had provided the only stable home life she had ever known. She continued to keep in touch with her father, who lived in Illinois, but they had never been very close. She expelled a sigh as she turned the page, knowing that if she did not get those Christmas displays set up pretty soon it would be too late to bother.

She took another sip of her coffee, but before she could swallow it, a photograph leaped off the page and grabbed her. The mug nearly slipped from her hand, spilling most of its contents on her newspaper. A hard gulp sent her swallow of hot coffee down the wrong way.

She fought the choking cough that spasmed in her throat as she tried to get her breath.

She could not believe her eyes. Right there in the newspaper, staring at her with that same devilish smile, was the man who had grabbed her on the street. He was with another man and the two of them were holding up a trophy. There was also a woman in the photograph, her arm linked through his, wearing a very skimpy bathing suit.

Marcie stared at the photograph again. There was no doubt about it. He was definitely the man whose kiss had gone right through her and even curled her toes. She had been trying to erase the incident from her mind, but to no avail. She closed her eyes for a moment as she recalled for perhaps the hundredth time every nuance of the heated instant when his lips had touched hers.

She scanned the caption beneath the photograph, then went back and carefully read it a second time. "Chance Fowler and Dave Stevens display their first place trophy from Saturday's regatta. This is the third win for Fowler and his racing sloop, *Celeste,* seen in the background."

"Chance Fowler." The words came out in

a hushed gasp, as if she were too stunned to even say the name. Chance Fowler? The man in the photograph was the one and only Chance Fowler? The man who had appeared from out of nowhere and totally swept her off her feet was the heir to the Fowler family fortune, the infamous playboy whose picture graced the pages of the tabloids as often as it did the society pages and sporting news?

Her brow wrinkled into a frown. She knew his type all too well—someone who refused to accept any responsibility and who could not make a commitment. She had once been engaged to a man who suddenly decided commitment was not for him. He had been convinced that marriage would tie him down to a dull daily routine. He wanted to be free to come and go as he wished. She had given him back his ring and told him to go follow his desires. When he said that he might be ready to settle down in a couple of years and in the meantime they could continue to date, she had told him to forget it.

When she married it would be to a man who wanted a stable home life, not someone who drifted from one adventure to another. She wanted somebody who would consider her to be an equal partner, an important part of his life. She did not want a relationship built around the idea that marriage and home was a burden to be endured because it was expected of you, something where you settled for less than what you wanted out of life.

Her father had been a dreamer who had always believed there was a greener pasture just over the next hill. He had pulled up stakes and moved the family so many times that she had not been able to spend more than a few months at a time in any one school. Her mother had finally sent her to live with her grandmother so she could have a secure home environment and attend all four years of high school at one place.

Her mother had died when Marcie was barely sixteen. She had never been very close to her father, his life-style leaving her with very definite opinions about responsibility, commitment, and what marriage should and should not be. And one thing it should not be was a union entered into with a man who could not commit to the responsibility of maintaining a stable and secure home life.

She glanced at the newspaper photograph again. The caption made no mention of the woman standing next to Chance Fowler, but from the way the woman was staring at him, it was obvious that they knew each other very well. She again noted the very skimpy bikini the woman was wearing. The woman looked exactly like the type she imagined he would be attracted to. ''Take-A-Chance Fowler,'' the tabloids had dubbed him. She touched her fingers to her lips. She could still feel the heat of his kiss even though she wished it was not so.

Marcie slowly sipped what little coffee remained in her mug, leaving the newspaper unread as she became totally absorbed in thought. Chance Fowler...never in a million years had she thought she would ever run into someone like him, but now that she had it was easy to understand why women vied for his attention. A ringing sound startled her out of her reverie.

She grabbed the cordless phone from the base station. ''Hello?''

''Marcie...it's Sandy. I'm afraid I won't be at work today. I've been awake most of the night with the stomach flu.''

It was not what Marcie wanted to hear. Sandy had been a dedicated employee for five years and had proven herself invaluable. Marcie had come to depend more and more on her.

"Okay, Sandy. I'll see you when you're feeling better."

"What about the wholesale flower mart in the morning?"

"Don't give it another thought. I'll take care of that. You just take care of yourself and get well."

"Thanks, Marcie. I'll call you tomorrow."

What Marcie had thought would be a leisurely day had suddenly turned into a very busy one. Saturday and Sunday were the busiest days for the nursery regardless of the time of year. Even though the flower shop was Sandy's primary domain, she usually helped out in the nursery on Sunday when the flower shop was closed. Marcie hurried through her shower and dressed for work. An hour later she was in the nursery preparing to open for the day's business.

A young man in his mid-twenties walked in the back door. "That does it, Marcie," he said as he removed his work gloves. "Everything's watered, dead leaves cut away, walkways all hosed down. I have Don restocking the wild bird feed right now. He's already straightened the bird feeder display and put out the two new birdhouse designs that came in a couple of days ago.''

''Thanks, Glen. As soon as Don's finished I'd like the two of you to move the planters on the north side to make room for the Christmas trees.''

Glen laughed as he wiped the perspiration from his forehead. ''Being from Michigan I still have a little trouble thinking in terms of Christmas without snow. And a Santa who arrives on water skis, wearing sunglasses and dressed in Bermuda shorts...well, that's definitely beyond my scope of reality.''

She smiled as she handed Glen an order form. ''Could you pull this order together sometime today? Mr. Adams's gardener is coming by to pick it up first thing in the morning.''

Glen took the order form. ''Sure.'' He offered her a weary smile that said they were not even open for business yet and already it had been a busy day. ''I'll get to it this afternoon.''

Glen was another one. Like Sandy, he was a dedicated employee Marcie had come to depend on. The expansion of the landscaping business had put an additional workload on the nursery employees. Sandy ran the flower shop and Marcie spent most of her time with the nursery, but Glen needed another person on the nursery payroll in addition to the four other employees who already worked under his supervision.

Marcie had run an ad a week earlier, but none of the applicants had measured up to what Glen considered suitable. He occasionally pulled one of the workers away from the landscaping crew when things got really backed up, but it was not an ideal situation. Glen had said he would rather work short-handed and know things were being done right than spend all his time following someone around, correcting sloppy work.

Marcie opened the nursery for business promptly at ten o'clock. There was a steady flow of customers in and out all day, keeping her very busy—but not too busy to prevent Chance Fowler from entering her thoughts again and again. It had been a random encounter, nothing more. She would not even have known who he was if his picture had not been in the newspaper that morning.

There was absolutely no reason for them to ever bump into each other again. They traveled in completely different circles. He lived in the heady realm of yacht clubs, world travel, and high-dollar society functions while she belonged to the world of backyard barbecues and walks on the beach. And even if they did meet again, there would be no reason for him to remember her. So why was she having so much difficulty exorcising him from her thoughts? She touched her fingertips to her lips, to the heat of his kiss—a gesture she had done so often the past couple of days that it had almost become a habit.

Marcie glanced at the clock—five-thirty. Another half hour and she could lock up the nursery and call it a day. She started bringing in the plants and various display items that had been placed outside the front entrance. She managed the smaller items by herself, then looked around for either Glen or Don. Neither employee was anywhere in sight, obviously busy in the greenhouse or out in back on the grounds. She shrugged, took a deep breath, and began struggling with a large planter.

Chance Fowler pulled into the parking lot of the Crestview Bay Nursery. A delightful sight caught his attention before he could even get out of his car. The woman who had refused to leave his thoughts stood next to the front entrance staring at a large redwood planter containing some sort of a bush. She circled the planter, pushed at it with her foot, then stood with her hands on her hips and stared at it. Finally she bent over and tried to pick it up.

He shoved open the car door, swung his long legs out, then quickly covered the distance to the front door of the nursery. Her back to him as she grappled with the task she had set for herself, Chance took a moment to visually trace each and every one of her curves with an appreciative gaze before stepping up behind her.

He put his arms around her to grab the planter as he whispered in her ear, "That looks heavy. Let me help you with it."

The words came from out of nowhere just as a pair of strong arms reached around her. She did not know which came first, her surprise or her recognition of *his* voice. She jerked upright, startled by his sudden intrusion, and whirled around to face him.

His uninhibited laugh filled the air. "Marcie Roper, I presume? You know, we really have to stop meeting like this." He gave her a quick wink followed by a mischievous grin. He glanced around as if to make sure no one could hear him, then lowered his voice to a conspiratorial whisper. ''If we don't watch out, the neighbors will start to gossip, then pretty soon everyone will know about our clandestine meetings in out-of-the-way places.''

Two

———

Marcie's eyes widened with shock. His devilish good looks, teasing grin, and tantalizing closeness momentarily drove every intelligent thought right out of her head. She quickly regained her composure. Just because he was the infamous Chance Fowler, it did not mean that he could get away with whatever he wanted. He had thrown her for a loop once with his aggressive and totally inappropriate behavior. She did not intend to allow him to do it again.

"You!" she snapped angrily, her words clipped. "What are you doing here? It's bad enough that you accosted me on the street and were responsible for my losing one of my packages. Was it also necessary for you to track me down and grab me like that...again? I don't care if your name is Chance Fowler, that doesn't give you the right to—''

He feigned a hurt expression. ''You helped me out of a tight spot. I was just trying to return the favor by helping you with the heavy planter.''

She glared at him, then placed her hands on her hips and leaned forward. She hoped her aggressive stance covered the out-of-control excitement that raced around inside her. Chance Fowler touched her and she seemed to lose all reason and logic—twice now.

''That doesn't explain your totally unac-ceptable behavior.'' She was determined to stand her ground no matter how tempting she found his touch or how much his presence made her heart pound.

He cocked his head and looked at her quiz-zically. ''It also doesn't explain how you knew who I was.''

''Humph!'' she snorted. The image of the bikini-clad woman hanging on his arm flashed in her mind. She was obviously typical of the type of woman he preferred—footloose and fancy free. ''Your picture was in today's news-paper in connection with the hobbies of the *pampered and privileged.''* She had not intended to reveal her disgust and disapproval of the idle rich in general, and specifically the life-style he had chosen for himself, but somehow her feelings had slipped past her words.

''Ah, yes, the regatta.'' He stared at her for a moment. Her eyes sparkled with the fire of emotion and her stance declared a very appealing independence. She was certainly different from the type of women he usually encountered. They were either insipid clinging vines or manipulative cloyers, and the result was always the same. He felt suffocated and trapped. Yes, indeed. Marcie Roper was quite different—a breath of fresh air. He recalled the way she had felt in his arms, the taste of her delicious mouth. He fought the almost overwhelming desire to pull her into his arms and kiss her again.

''Speaking of newspapers, I'd like to explain about last Friday. There was this tabloid photographer who spotted me and—''

''I really don't care *why* it happened, Mr. Fowler. The fact is that it should not have happened at all. You had no right to grab me like that...no right at all. Maybe that kind of intrusion is normal behavior for your friends, but it certainly isn't for me.''

Marcie caught a glimpse of Don out of the corner of her eye and turned her attention toward him. ''Don, could you move the rest of these things inside?'' She shot a quick glance in Chance's direction, then continued her instructions. She carefully and deliberately chose her words. ''Since we don't have any customers, we might as well go ahead and close up.''

She threw Chance one last disagreeable look, turned her back to him and went inside the nursery. A moment later she began the closing procedures for the day.

Chance watched her walk away from him— for the second time since he'd first encountered her. She had turned out to be a very intriguing woman. He already knew about the golden flecks in her hazel eyes, her soft, pliable lips, her addictive taste, and how good she felt in his arms. And now he could add strong-willed, independent, outspoken, and deliciously tempting to that list.

As with most people who did not know him, she had categorized him according to tabloid misinformation and exaggeration. He seldom allowed such misconceptions to bother him.

He knew who he was, as did the small group of people he counted as his true friends and work associates. He rarely felt the need to explain himself to strangers. Only with Marcie did he find himself in a bit of a quandary.

He had never been one to back down from a challenge, and Marcie Roper certainly fit in that category. He could still see the intense glare she had leveled at him before turning away. No one had ever told him to go to hell so emphatically without uttering a word. She was unlike any other woman he had ever met. He followed her inside the building, determined to learn more about this fascinating and desirable woman.

Marcie grabbed up a stack of receipts and credit card slips. She could not believe the audacity of Chance Fowler—the man's arrogance was beyond anything she had ever encountered. It was obvious that he was accustomed to getting whatever he wanted. Well, he was not going to get away with that sort of high-handed behavior around her. She paused for a moment as she once again touched her fingertips to her lips. His kiss was also beyond anything she had ever experienced.

"About that little incident the other day... I'd like to make it up to you."

His smooth voice broke into her moment of reflection. She looked up, surprised that he had followed her inside. She quickly pulled her composure together, meeting his captivating gaze with a cool one of her own. "Are you still here?"

He refused to allow her the upper hand. Besides, he had not yet played his trump card. He made an exaggerated show of glancing around, as if attempting to seek out something, then returned his attention to her. "Yep...as near as I can tell, I'm still here."

His response seemed to fluster her. Her gaze darted around the room. He stood his ground and waited, refusing to say anything to relieve her obvious discomfort. He had to admit, if only to himself, that he was enjoying the moment.

"Well, uh, unless you plan to buy something, I'll have to ask you to leave. We're closing for the day." She returned her attention to the receipts on the counter.

"In that case, I guess I'll have to buy something." He flashed her a teasing grin and gave her a quick wink before turning away from the counter. He surveyed the room for a moment, then inspected the items available for sale. He did not look back at her, even though the temptation was almost too much to resist. He fought the grin that tugged at the corners of his mouth as he picked up a bird feeder and examined it.

"I'll take this." He placed the feeder on the counter in front of her. He looked up, capturing her gaze and intimately holding it for a moment. He felt the warmth suffuse his body. He felt something else, too—a stirring that told him this was more than just a game. This woman had an effect on him far greater than he wanted to admit.

Relationships, commitment...he cynically reminded himself that it was all a sham. He had seen too many bad marriages to believe otherwise, not the least of which had been his father's four subsequent wives after divorcing his mother. No man should be married five times. And with his father's track record there was no reason to believe that the fifth ex-Mrs. Douglas Fowler—a woman who had been relegated to the position after only one year of marriage—would be the last one.

Not liking the path his thoughts seemed to

be taking, Chance forced the distasteful topic from his mind.

"What kind of birds will I get with this feeder?"

Marcie made every effort to keep the conversation all-business. She also made no effort to be civil about it. "None, unless you buy some bird feed to go with it."

"What would you recommend?" He was determined to prolong their meeting, as determined as she seemed to be to end it.

She brushed a loose tendril of hair away from her face. Her voice revealed her impatience with him. "Really, Mr. Fowler, is this conversation necessary? Don't you have something *important* you should be doing someplace else?"

"I find *this* to be something important." The words, soft and sincere, had slipped out without him meaning for them to. He quickly recovered his breezy facade. "As you said, the bird feeder is no good without something to go inside it. So—" he reached for a ten-pound sack of wild bird feed "—is this what I need?"

"Yes." Her reply was curt. She did not intend to waste any more time on him by discussing the merits of one type of feed over another. She just wanted him to leave. "Will that be cash or charge?"

"Cash."

He pulled his wallet from his pocket while she rang up the sale. She took his money, gave him his change, then placed the items in a box and shoved them across the counter toward him.

She tried to sound as cool and confident as she could even though her stomach churned and her nerve endings tingled with a surge of excitement when she caught a whiff of his aftershave. "Goodbye, Mr. Fowler."

"Goodbye?" He leaned forward, pressing the palms of his hands against the counter. He lowered his voice to a soft, intimate level. "I thought maybe we could have a drink when you finished here. It would allow me to apologize…and give us an opportunity to get to know each other better."

It took all the fortitude she could muster to fix him with a stern look. "I believe we know each other as well as we need to. Goodbye, Mr. Fowler."

He refused to be put off. It was definitely time for that trump card. He picked up the box containing his purchases and flashed a devastating smile. "I'll see you later, Marcie Roper."

She stared at his retreating form, her mouth hanging open in stunned silence. Even though she had accused him of tracking her down, she had been so startled by his sudden appearance that it had not occurred to her to ask him how he knew her name or where to find her. She started to call after him, but quickly closed her mouth. Nothing would be gained by making him think she had any interest in his detective skills.

She watched as he left the nursery and crossed the parking lot to his car, every step and gesture indicative of a man who knew exactly who he was, where he was going, and what he wanted out of life. She hurried to lock the front door and put out the Closed sign. She paused for a moment and took a deep breath in an attempt to restore some semblance of order to the shambles his presence had made of her routine.

She returned to the cash register and began ringing up the totals for the day's business. The sound of someone tapping against the front window drew her attention away from her work. She looked up to see Chance Fowler motioning for her to let him in. She shook her head and mouthed the words, "We're closed," while pointing to the sign.

He tapped on the window again and triumphantly displayed his hidden prize. He held up the sack so she could see it.

Marcie squinted as she stared at the object, at first not understanding the significance it held. Then the words came into focus—the sack was from the bookstore where she had picked up her order the day Chance Fowler had turned her life upside down. Could it possibly be the bag she had lost? She furrowed her brow in confusion as she made her way toward the door.

Again he motioned for her to unlock the door and let him in. She hesitated for a moment, then complied with his wishes…to a certain extent. She unlocked and opened the door, but did not stand aside to allow him entry. She stared at the sack without reaching for it, then shifted her gaze to him as her curiosity outweighed her impatience. "I'm really very busy right now, Mr. Fowler. Just what is it you want?"

"I believe I have something here that belongs to you. May I come in?"

She hesitated, then stepped aside.

Chance walked across the room and placed the bag on the counter. "You dropped this the other day. I tried to follow you to return it, but by the time I got to the corner you had disappeared." He reached into the sack, withdrew the sales slip and placed it on the counter. "Fortunately, this had your name on it."

She picked up the sales receipt and looked at it, then took the books from the bag. Her voice grew soft, conveying just a hint of embarrassment as she inspected the contents. "I—I thought they were lost for good. This one—" she held up the large volume about the Civil War "—is a birthday present for my father." She ran her fingertips across the cover of the book, then looked up at the very handsome man standing on the other side of the counter.

Her manner softened considerably. "Thank you for returning my books." Her words were unquestionably sincere.

"I'm just glad that I was able to track you down. I thought it was the least I could do in light of the fact that it was probably my fault that you dropped them." Her shy smile captured and held him as tightly as if she had physically put her arms around him. A little twinge of longing told him it was an idea that he found very appealing—and definitely an idea worth pursuing. The memory of her taste and how she had felt in his arms told him there was no way he was going to let this just drift away like so many other things in his life.

"Well..." She glanced down, then looked up at him again. "Anyway, it was nice of you to go to all of this trouble. I really appreciate the gesture."

"Enough to have dinner with me tonight?" He saw the way she stiffened in response to his invitation. The shy softness that had covered her features just a second earlier had changed into wariness.

"That's impossible." Her words were clipped, indicating her displeasure. "I have an employee out sick, so I need to be at the San Diego wholesale flower mart at five o'clock in the morning. That doesn't allow me the luxury of socializing tonight." She hurried toward the front door and held it open for him. "Thank you, again, for returning my books. Good night."

Chance hesitated a moment. There did not seem to be anything to say that would change the situation, so he acquiesced to her wishes. "Good night, Marcie Roper." He flashed a devilish smile that said she would definitely be seeing him again. "Pleasant dreams."

Marcie watched as he crossed the parking lot to his car. The audacity of the man. Her disgust sounded loud and clear in her thoughts. He was obviously accustomed to thinking everyone would simply drop whatever they were doing to cater to his whims. Well, he had another think coming where she was concerned. Unlike other people, she was not impressed with whom he was.

Her fingertips lightly touched her lips. No matter what she tried to tell herself, she could not shake the very real sensuality of his kiss. He personified everything she found unacceptable, yet she was unable to dismiss him from her mind.

Pleasant dreams, indeed! She returned to her close-out chores as she made yet another unsuccessful attempt at shoving Chance Fowler from her thoughts.

The gray streaks of predawn light had not yet penetrated the black sky when Marcie pulled the nursery van out of the parking lot and headed south toward San Diego. She stifled a yawn, then reached for her travel mug of coffee. The night had been far too short, the alarm jarring her awake way too early. She had gone to bed in plenty of time to get enough sleep…if she had been able to sleep. As much as she tried to ignore it, however, thoughts and images of Chance Fowler kept circulating through her mind.

Regardless of how attractive she found him and how much he heated her desires, she knew nothing would be gained from speculating about where things might have led if she had accepted his initial invitation to join him for a drink, or his later offer to have dinner with him. He was an irresponsible, headline-grabbing playboy who did not know the first thing about hard work and commitment. That was everything she knew about him and it was everything she needed to know.

She drained the last swallow from her coffee mug just as she pulled into the flower mart. She parked the van, locked the door, then hurried inside to make her purchases. She stifled another yawn. It was going to be a very long day.

Chance glanced at his watch. Five forty-five in the morning was a wretched time to be up, but some things were worth a little extra sacrifice. He spotted the nursery van as soon as he pulled into the parking lot and he quickly secured a parking space for himself. After spending a restless night in an unsuccessful attempt to shove the memory of Marcie Roper's taste and feel from his mind he had come to the conclusion that she was definitely one of those exceptions among women—at least the ones he knew—and it was definitely worth a great deal of effort on his part to get to know her better.

There was something special about her that reached out to him, something that made a direct connection to the place inside him that yearned for more than his relationships of the past had brought him. The kiss they had shared told him there was a very sensual woman beneath that practical exterior. He did not intend to let her slip away.

He wandered around for a bit, surprised at all the activity taking place at that hour of the morning. He finally spotted Marcie. He paused for a moment as he watched her signing something and handing it back to a sales clerk. He studied the way she moved, the way her clothes fit her body, the delicate features surrounded by the softly feathered auburn curls. He took a deep breath in an effort to break the tightness that banded his chest. No other woman had ever affected him in quite this manner and he found it very perplexing—and far too disturbingly real.

He saw her struggle with a large flatbed cart stacked with boxes and he hurried to assist her.

"Let me help you with that." He immediately took control of maneuvering the unwieldy cart as if there were nothing unusual about him being there. He purposely ignored her shocked expression as he pushed the cart in the direction she had been heading.

He kept the conversation light and upbeat. "I'm experiencing a strange sensation of having helped you move something heavy once before...almost as if it were only yesterday." He turned toward her and flashed a teasing grin. "How about you? Have you ever had similar feelings of déjà vu?"

"What are you doing here?"

"I thought it was obvious. I'm helping you with your cart." He reached down and opened one of the boxes, pausing a moment as he inspected the contents. He looked at her questioningly. "Fresh-cut flowers?"

"Hardly unusual since this is the wholesale flower mart and I do own a flower shop."

"Yes, but you also have a nursery." He replaced the lid on the box and steered the cart slowly along the aisle.

She walked with him, still not clear as to why he was there or what he wanted. "One has nothing to do with the other. Cut flowers and floral arrangements are a different business from plants and landscaping."

He extended a warm smile. "That's gratifying."

She wrinkled her brow in confusion. "What's gratifying?"

"Learning something new is gratifying, even at this horrible hour of the morning."

"Isn't this a little too early for someone like you to be up?" She detected the sarcasm that surrounded her words, but seemed to be unable to stop it. "Or are you still up from last night?"

He stopped the cart and leaned against the

handle, cocking his head and raising an eye-
brow as he leveled a steady gaze in her direction. He hid behind a neutral mask, his expression revealing almost no hint of what was
going through his mind. Only the slightest in-
dication of discomfort darted through his eyes,
almost as if he had flinched in reaction to a
physical attack.

She immediately regretted her words. It had
been uncalled for and unnecessary. His eyes
were clear and alert, rather than bloodshot, and
he appeared rested. He certainly did not look
as if he had been up partying all night.

She glanced down at the floor, then regained
eye contact with him. A tickle of embarrassment immediately caught hold. ''I—I'm sorry.
It was unfair of me to have said that.''

''Yes, it was unfair.'' There was no anger
in his voice nor was there any hostility attached to his words. There was, however, a
hint of puzzlement. ''What made you do it?''

''Well...'' Anxiety churned in the pit of her
stomach. He had every right to be angry with
her, but he seemed more hurt than anything
else. ''You do have to admit that you have a
certain reputation.'' She felt the heat of her
embarrassment flush across her cheeks as she

continued to speak. "Heir to the family fortune, member of the privileged elite...well-known playboy."

"You make it sound as if being born to wealthy parents is some sort of sin, or worse yet, a terrible disease."

"I didn't mean for it to sound that way. It's just that your exploits have been pretty thoroughly documented by the press—"

"Oh?" He started walking again, pushing the heavy cart in front of him. "You're a fan of the tabloids?"

"No. I mean, well...I sometimes glance at the headlines while standing in the checkout line at the grocery store, but so does everyone else."

"You believe everything you read in the newspapers?"

"Well, no...but—"

"I see." A hint of annoyance crept into his voice. "*Normally* you wouldn't believe everything you read, but you decided to make an exception in my case."

Marcie knew his words were true and justified, but they did not alter her opinion. "We're obviously different types of people, that's all. You have your life-style and I have mine.''

''You make 'life-style' sound like some sort of affliction.'' An amused twinkle danced through his eyes and a mischievous grin tugged at the corners of his mouth. ''I can see that I need to do some serious damage control here.''

He paused a moment as his attention moved to more immediate matters. ''Where are we going with this?''

''Where are we going with what?'' Was he talking about their conversation? Their situation? He had moved from annoyed to amused to...she did not know what, in less than sixty seconds. She was not sure exactly what he was talking about.

''Where are we going with this cart? We're almost to the door. Are you through or do you have more to do here?''

''I'm finished. I've already charged this to my account. So—'' she grabbed the handle to take charge of the cart ''—thank you for your assistance. I can manage it from here.''

He refused to move aside. ''I'll help you out with these boxes.'' He shoved the cart through the check out area, moving quickly as he headed toward her van.

She hurried after Chance, not sure exactly when it was that she had lost control, or exactly when he had managed to take charge. "Wait a minute." She caught up with his fast-paced stride. She tried to sound assertive. "Really, Mr. Fowler, I can handle the rest of this by myself."

Chance ignored her words. He pushed the cart next to the van, tried the door, then held out his hand toward her. "Keys?"

Marcie hesitated a moment, then unlocked the door for him. A couple of minutes later he had all the boxes off the cart and loaded inside the van. He leaned against the side of the vehicle, noting the way she nervously shifted her weight from one foot to the other.

During the course of their three encounters she had run away from him, ignored him, been rude to him, rejected his invitations and cast aspersions on his character. And still he could not tear himself away from her. He certainly was not a masochist nor was he so desperate for feminine companionship that he needed to put up with this type of treatment to spend a little bit of time with an attractive woman.

There was no logical reason for him to be standing there, but somehow this woman had reached out and grabbed hold of his senses as no one else ever had. She was her own woman, not what she thought someone else wanted her to be. She had her identity intact, unlike most of the women he knew who would rather attach themselves to his. It was a very appealing aspect of who she was. She was also intelligent, beautiful, independent—*very* independent. He could still feel her body enfolded in his embrace and taste her mouth pressed against his. She was everything a man could want.

"Well..." She nervously shifted her weight from one foot to the other. "If you'll excuse me—"

He offered an inviting smile. "Let's go get some coffee."

"That's not possible, Mr. Fowler. These are cut flowers, not plants. I need to get them back to the shop immediately and put them in the cooler."

"Okay. We can get some coffee after you take care of the flowers. And please, call me Chance. *Mr. Fowler* is reserved for dear ol'

Dad, the one and only Douglas Winston Fowler.''

She stiffened to attention, literally as well as figuratively. ''I don't believe I'd feel comfortable calling you by some cute little nickname given to you by the press... 'Take-A-Chance Fowler,' always ready to take a chance on some new adventure...''

Her words trailed off when she saw that look dart through his eyes, the same one she had seen when she had called him a playboy. Only this time it did not disappear as quickly as it had before.

He looked away from her for a moment, as if collecting his thoughts, then recaptured eye contact with her. ''Chance is my legal first name, given to me at birth. It was my mother's maiden name.''

A stab of guilt caught her up short when she saw his reaction to her words mirrored in his eyes. It was almost as if she had reached out and physically struck him. She spoke with genuine regret as she tried to apologize. ''I—I'm sorry. I didn't know.''

He glanced away again before saying, his voice soft, ''It doesn't matter.''

She heard what he said, but she did not believe him. She could tell that it did matter, that it mattered very much. Without meaning to, she had hurt him and she felt bad about it. "I just assumed—"

"You seem to assume a lot."

Chance had said the words without malice or anger, but he had not been able to hide the underlying vulnerability that seeped into his tone of voice. Marcie felt the pangs of guilt stab deep inside her. She knew she had been less than gracious. That was a laugh—she had been downright rude. Something about this quick glimpse of the man beneath the facade touched an emotional place for her. It was a different place than the excitement caused by his kiss. This was a place of caring, tenderness, and concern. She took a deep breath, held it for a moment, then slowly expelled it.

"You're right." The sharp edge to her voice was gone, along with her guarded attitude. "I sometimes do tend to make assumptions. It's a bad habit of mine." An additional softness caressed her next words. "I apologize for the crack about your name. It was totally uncalled for."

"I'll tell you what, Marcie Roper." He reached out and ran his fingertips across her cheek, then cupped her chin in his hand. He plumbed the depths of her eyes. He saw uncertainty, wariness, and something else…a warmth and a passion that he very much wanted to tap into. He quickly allowed his hand to drop away as the temptation to kiss her grew stronger. ''You can make it up to me by joining me for a drink when you get off work tonight.''

She glanced down at the ground, indecision churning inside her. ''I—I don't know.''

''Now that's what I call an improvement— you didn't reject my invitation outright. You've left it open for discussion.'' He placed his fingertips underneath her chin again and gently raised her face until he could look into her eyes. ''Why don't we try for the next level, where you agree to have dinner with me this evening?''

''You're certainly a fast worker.'' A shy smile turned up the corners of her mouth. ''A minute ago it was coffee, then it became a drink after work, and now it's dinner tonight.''

''You should have accepted my invitation at the coffee level. Now, it's too late. Besides, you owe me.'' He saw her objection start to form, and quickly cut it off before she could give it a voice. "You owe me the opportunity to prove that your preconceived notions about me are wrong."

He flashed a teasing grin. "Surely you wouldn't deny me my Constitutional right of being innocent until proven guilty..." His smile faded as he searched out her vulnerability and caressed the essence of her soul. "Would you?"

"I suppose I do owe you that much." There was a hint of concern surrounding Marcie's words. She was not sure exactly how she had gotten herself into this predicament.

"Good." Chance's face literally beamed his pleasure at her acceptance. "When will you be finished with work? What time should I pick you up? And where—at the nursery or at your house?"

"No... I mean, it would be more convenient if I met you somewhere." The last thing she wanted was to be trapped someplace where she could not conveniently and quickly leave if things turned out the way she feared they probably would. She caught herself, putting an immediate stop to the direction her thoughts were taking her. She was making assumptions again.

He had been correct, it was a bad habit. It was something she needed to work on.

He hesitated a moment, then gave in to her request. "All right. How about the Crestview Bay Bistro? The food there is good, the atmosphere comfortable, and the ocean view is terrific."

"Sure, that will be fine." She wondered if he had picked the bistro as a convenience for her since it was close to the nursery, or if it was someplace he really wanted to go. "What time?"

"You tell me... I don't know your work schedule."

She thought a moment. With Sandy out sick she would not be able to get away early. "How about seven o'clock? Will that be okay?"

He flashed a smile of genuine pleasure. "That will be absolutely perfect. I'll make reservations." He reached for her hand and gave it a little squeeze—not what he wanted to do, but it would have to suffice for the moment. "I'll see you tonight."

She watched him shove the cart toward the collection point outside the main entrance of the building. A hint of anxiety churned in her stomach. She quickly climbed into her van and headed out of the parking lot before he could return. She had made the commitment to have dinner with him. She was obligated to show up. Another hint of anxiety shuddered through her body. It was not trepidation. She was certainly not afraid of him. But it was anxiety none the less. Could it be her own feelings and emotions that she feared? It was an unanswered question that did not sit well with her.

Chance returned to his car just in time to see Marcie pull out of the parking lot. He was not sure exactly why he was so attracted to her, beyond the obvious of her being a very enticing woman. Was it merely the challenge of charming someone who kept rejecting him, or did it go much deeper than the shallowness of a physical attraction? He was not really sure he wanted to know the answer to that question, but the possibilities definitely disturbed him and at the same time they excited him.

For the first time in his life he seemed to be treading a thin line between playing a game and being drawn into what could only end up as a serious relationship. There was no doubt in his mind that with Marcie it could never be a casual affair. She was not the type of woman who would be willing to play games just for the fun of it. No matter how many times he told himself to get out and move on to something that was less of a threat, he did not seem to be able to do it.

Three

Chance arrived at the bistro nearly half an hour early. He secured a quiet table in a corner of the cocktail lounge and ordered a beer. It had been a bad day all around, starting with the insistent ringing of his phone as he arrived home from the flower mart.

The phone call had been from Hank Varney, apprising him that one of his students had gotten into trouble again. He had to admit that he was not surprised about Jeff being picked up for car theft, but it still upset him more than he wanted to admit. He knew he could not expect to have a one hundred percent success rate with the program, but when one of his students turned to criminal ways, Chance always took it personally.

Which brought him to another point of contention between Chance and his father. When he'd first come up with the plan to take school dropouts, disadvantaged older teens, and those who were having a difficult time of it because of an arrest record for minor offenses, and teach them a trade so they could make it in the world, his father had been vehemently against it.

"Can't trust these punks... They'll rob you blind... There will be no sponsorship from any of my companies." His father's words rang loud and clear in his ears, even five years later. That had been the last time he had attempted to talk to his father about it. Chance had gone ahead on his own and implemented his ideas, only on a smaller scale. He had formed a non-profit organization, then established a working relationship with two contractors, one in San Diego and the other in San Francisco, where Chance maintained a second home.

It had taken all his charm and persuasive powers to convince the city and state officials whose agencies could recommend candidates for his program that he was sincere about wanting to help. It had been the largest hurdle for him—getting them to see him as something other than a spoiled son of a wealthy and powerful man, who was only playing at having a social conscience.

Chance bought fixer-upper houses and his students, under the supervision of a licensed contractor, did the repairs and remodeling. Once the property was sold, the profits were used to finance the next project, including wages for the students. The contractors would then work the graduating students into their respective construction crews as fully paid employees.

For the past five years everything had gone pretty much according to plan. But every now and then one of his students made a grab for what seemed like easy money rather than perform hard work. He had had such high hopes for Jeff, so it was with a heavy heart that he had left the jail that afternoon after talking to him. There had been no remorse on Jeff's part, only arrogance and defiance. Chance's failures were few and far between, but this particular one had upset him more than the others.

He continued to ponder the unfortunate turn of circumstances as he sipped his beer. Jeff's arrest was not the only upsetting news of the day. He had received an e-mail just before leaving home to meet Marcie for dinner. He unfolded the printout and stared at it again.

Marcie arrived at the Bistro promptly at seven o'clock. She had barely found enough time to go home, take a quick turn through the shower, and change clothes. She spotted Chance seated by himself in the corner of the cocktail lounge. He seemed to be studying a piece of paper. The pensive expression on his face said he was troubled about something. She watched him for a moment before crossing the room to his table.

"Good evening."

Chance looked up at the intrusion into his thoughts. As soon as he saw Marcie he rose to his feet and extended a warm smile. "Hello." He took in the way the soft fabric of her blouse caressed her breasts, how her skirt accentuated her slim waist and the sleek curve of her calf. He glanced at his watch. "I didn't realize it was seven o'clock already. I'll get us a table for dinner."

They were seated in the dining room at a nice table next to a window with an ocean view. Chance looked at the wine list while Marcie studied the menu. He gave their selections to the waiter, then settled back in his chair. He studied her for a moment. She appeared nervous, continually glancing around the room and out the window.

"You look very nice. Your blouse is a good color for you. It really brings out your eyes." He leaned forward. "And you have lovely eyes."

She could feel the flush of embarrassment spread across her cheeks and the butterflies dance in her stomach. She hoped her voice did not sound as unsettled as she felt. "You're very good at this…knowing just the right thing to say at just the proper moment. But then, I imagine you get lots of practice."

An amused grin tugged at the corners of his mouth. "There you go again…making assumptions. I think you have lovely eyes, so I told you so. It was a simple compliment, nothing devious or subversive about it."

The waiter brought the bottle of wine Chance had ordered, poured each of them a glass, then left. Marcie took a sip of her wine, then toyed with the stem of the wineglass and ran her finger around the rim. The lull in the conversation felt awkward to her. Agreeing to have dinner with him had been a bad idea. They obviously had nothing in common.

She nervously cleared her throat. She felt pressured to say something—anything—to break the uncomfortable silence. "When I arrived, you had such an intense look on your face I was reluctant to interrupt your concentration. I hope it wasn't some sort of problem or bad news."

"Well..." He took a drink from his glass. "I guess you could call it the perfect capper to a day of problems."

She allowed a bit of a chuckle. "Starting with getting up at such a horrible hour this morning?"

He extended a sincere smile. "Not at all." He reached across the table and covered her hand with his. His gaze settled on her face, then delved into her eyes. His voice was low, his words cloaked in honesty. "That was the best part of my entire day...until now."

Her gaze shifted away from him as she eased her hand out from beneath his. She picked up her wineglass and took another sip, then feigned an interest in something out the window.

"It's certainly a nice evening." She heard the strain in her voice as she attempted to make polite conversation. When he did not respond to what she had said, she turned her gaze back to him. He had the same pensive expression on his face as he'd had when she'd first spotted him in the cocktail lounge. He seemed a million miles away in thought. Again, she was not sure if she should disturb him or not.

"Uh, Chance…is something wrong? You seem troubled."

His head snapped up to attention at the sound of his name. He had been so absorbed in his thoughts that he had neglected to hear what she had been saying. He let out a sigh of exasperation as he leaned back in his chair. "Sorry… As I said earlier, it's been a really lousy day."

"Is there anything I can do to help?" A sudden wave of shy embarrassment swept over her. "I—I'm sorry, I didn't mean to intrude. It's obviously none of my business."

"That's all right." A hint of weariness clouded his features for a second. He did not want to talk about Jeff's arrest. His activities with his "training school," as he referred to it, were something he kept to himself. But the e-mail he had received from his father was an entirely different matter. He pulled the printout from his pocket and handed it to her. "I'm sure it will be in the newspapers in the morning anyway."

She unfolded and read the piece of paper. It was a message from Douglas Fowler to his son stating that he had gotten married the day before and had left that morning and would be honeymooning on the French Riviera for the next ten days. She handed it back to him.

The look of confusion on her face told Chance that she did not understand the significance of the message.

"It's not that dear ol' Dad has decided to get married again without even bothering to invite his one and only son to the wedding, it's that this is his sixth trip down the aisle. The fifth Mrs. Douglas Fowler lasted less than a year."

"You're kidding!" She could not hide her surprise. "Your father has been married six times?"

A chuckle escaped his throat. It was not a sound of amusement, but one of bittersweet irony. "This one is younger than I am. Care to make any bets on how long she'll last?"

"Why in the world would anyone want to get married six times?"

"That's an excellent question. Unfortunately I don't have even a mediocre answer let alone a good one." His brow furrowed for a moment, then he flashed an easy smile. "I guess everyone has to have a hobby, and getting married is his." He tried to sound casual, but somehow it did not quite come out that way. "You see, my family is more akin to life mirroring satire rather than the other way around."

His smile faded, to be replaced by a look of melancholy. He stared out the window, his gaze unfocused, his words seemingly meant more for himself than for her. "It has taught me one very important thing, though—marriage isn't worth the certificate it's printed on."

"That's rather a cynical attitude, isn't it?"

His attention snapped back to her, the look on his face saying she had caught him off guard almost as if he had not realized he had spoken his thoughts out loud. "You think so? How do you see it?"

"What about your mother?" Marcie could not believe how brazen she was being with her questions. It was not like her to pry into someone else's business, especially someone who was virtually a stranger, but she could not help herself. It was another glimpse past the facade and into the real Chance Fowler.

"Ah, the first Mrs. Douglas Fowler." His features softened and the sharp edge left his voice. "My mother died fifteen years ago, just a few days after my twenty-first birthday. I can't imagine how she and my father ever got together. Other than being members of the same social set and coming from the same type of economic background, they really had nothing personal in common. Mother valued family and friends. She believed in giving back rather than just taking." The hard edge returned to his tone. "And Dad prizes money, power, and winning above everything else."

Her next question was tentative, as if she were almost afraid to ask it. "And what about you? What do you value?"

Their gazes locked for a long moment enhanced by an intimate warmth that permeated the space between them. Then the waiter arrived with their dinner, and her question went unanswered.

They enjoyed what to Marcie's surprise

turned out to be a very pleasant meal. They lingered over coffee as they chatted amiably about safe topics such as movies, television, and books. The time passed quickly. She knew her senses had been muddled by Chance Fowler, but she refused to admit that she had succumbed to the mesmerizing spell of this dynamic man. She was far too sensible to let some headline-grabbing playboy turn her head regardless of how charming she found him...or how much she could still feel the heat of his kiss. At least, that was what she tried to tell herself.

Chance paid the check, then held Marcie's chair for her as she rose to her feet. He placed his hand gently at the small of her back and guided her toward the door. As soon as they were outside she paused a moment, closed her eyes, and filled her lungs with the cool ocean air.

"Mmm...that smells good. I was beginning to get a little drowsy in the restaurant. This night air is just the thing to perk me up."

"I certainly didn't mean to bore you."

She whirled around to face him, her voice containing a hint of urgency and concern. "Oh, no...I didn't mean to imply—" His impish grin and the teasing glint in his eyes stopped her in midsentence.

She returned his smile. "Dinner was very nice. Thank you."

The moonlight shimmered off the ocean and bathed the night in a silvery glow. A gentle breeze ruffled through her hair. "Thank you for sharing it with me." His voice caressed her senses as softly as the sound of the breaking waves whispering in the background. "I enjoyed it, too."

He cupped her chin in his hand, then leaned his face into hers, placing a gentle kiss on her lips. It lasted only a couple of seconds, but it was long enough to ignite all the sparks of the original kiss.

Marcie found the tender moment to be surprisingly free of any awkwardness. Even more surprising to her was her awareness of the subtle shift in her attitude where Chance Fowler was concerned. He had allowed her a glimpse beyond his public persona, albeit a very brief one, but it was enough for her to know there was a lot more substance to him than she had originally given him credit for.

He took her hand in his and they walked toward her car in silence. As soon as she slid in behind the steering wheel, he leaned over and asked, "Would it be presumptuous of me to invite myself back to your house for an after-dinner drink?"

She hesitated for a moment, then raised her arm to look at her watch. He quickly covered her watch with his hand. "It's not really that late and I promise I won't stay long."

"Well…" She felt herself being pulled in by the magnetic force of his undeniable sex appeal and her very real attraction to him.

"It's been such a nice evening, I hate to see it end so early." He brushed another soft kiss against her lips.

"I suppose it will be okay…" She took in a calming breath in an attempt to still the shiver of excitement that suddenly tickled across her skin. "For a few minutes."

She drove home and he followed her in his car. She lived in a small house in an older but neatly cared for neighborhood a few blocks from the nursery. She unlocked the front door and they entered the living room.

"Make yourself comfortable while I pour us a glass of wine."

Marcie went to the kitchen while Chance looked around. The tastefully decorated room radiated a comfortable warmth, reflecting the personality of the woman who lived there. It was more than merely a house, it was a home. He maintained two residences, the condominium he owned in San Francisco and his house in San Diego. But he didn't consider either of them a real home. It was one more clue that told him with Marcie Roper it would be all or nothing.

A stab of trepidation jabbed at his insides. He shook away the disconcerting feeling as he glanced down the hallway at what appeared to be two bedrooms and a bathroom. He wandered into the dining room and looked out the back window to the patio, then went to the kitchen.

He met her at the kitchen door. She handed him a glass of wine and carried her glass to the living room, pausing to turn on the stereo to a soft music station.

"I see you have a fireplace and I noticed some firewood stacked on your back patio. I could build a fire." It was a calculated move on his part. A fire would last longer than a glass of wine and would allow him to stay later.

"No. I mean, I think it's too late to start a

fire this evening.'' Anxiety jittered through her stomach. She could imagine herself folded in his embrace and his lips burning against hers with the same intensity as when he had grabbed her on the street. What she could not imagine was what had prompted her to agree to let him come back to her house for a drink…or what future there could be in pursuing the possibility of a relationship with Chance Fowler.

She sat in the large easy chair, partly because it was comfortable, but mostly to prevent him from sitting next to her. He settled in at the end of the sofa.

''These photographs—'' He gestured toward the many framed pictures decorating the walls. ''Did you take them?''

''Yes, they're my work.''

''They're quite good.''

''Thank you. I took some photography classes in college. At one time I thought it might be a fun career to be a photojournalist and work for a *National Geographic*-type magazine.'' A hint of yearning, possibly signaling a moment of regret, crept into her voice. ''But it really wasn't for me. I inherited enough money from my grandmother to purchase the nursery and I've been here ever since. This is the house my grandmother and I lived in for several years.''

He cocked his head and studied her for a moment. ''Did you ever feel that you missed out on something? That you should have pursued the challenge rather than settle for something else?''

Her defensiveness leaped to the forefront in response to his comment. ''I don't feel that I've *settled,* as you put it. I'm happy here. I like what I do. Besides, having a stable home and solid roots is very important to me.''

''I didn't mean to imply that you weren't content with the choice you had made. I was just wondering why you chose not to go with the photography. Judging from what I see here, I think you could have been very successful at it.''

She allowed her gaze to move from photograph to photograph, lingering for a moment with each picture and what it meant to her. ''Well, that's not the way it worked out.'' A hint of wistfulness covered her words.

''You know about my sad family tale, so how about telling me about your family? I know your father apparently enjoys books about the Civil War and that you lived with your grandmother. What about your mother? Any brothers or sisters?''

''I was an only child. My mother died when I was in high school. I, uh, was raised mostly by my grandmother. My parents traveled around a lot...it was my father's work...well, my mother thought it would be better for me—''

He saw her squirm uneasily in her chair and noted the way her gaze darted from place to place without really settling on anything. Then she rose and moved around the room, straightening things that did not need to be straightened, her movements awkward and unnatural. There was no question in his mind that she was uncomfortable with the conversation. He understood and respected her apparent feelings in the matter. He usually felt ill at ease whenever a conversation turned to his personal life and family. Perhaps it was something they had in common, but he would save it for another time.

He noticed her attempt to stifle a yawn. She had been at the flower mart at five that morning and then had worked all day. It was not surprising that she was sleepy. ''I'm keeping you up. I'd better get out of here so you can get some sleep.'' He rose from the sofa and carried his empty wineglass to the kitchen, placing it on the counter.

Marcie stifled another yawn, then extended a shy smile of apology. ''It's been a very long day for me.'' She felt the conflicting emotions churning inside her. She knew having him leave was the best thing. He simply was not the type of man she needed or wanted in her life. She had worked too hard building up a business with a good name for quality and reliability within the community. It would not be to her advantage for her company to be linked with someone whose name and picture periodically graced the pages of the tabloids.

But then, there was the excitement that jittered inside her whenever they came in physical contact...and the all too real memory of the sensual heat of his kiss. She clenched her jaw for a moment as her inner resolve took hold. She would not allow her life to be ruled by a physical attraction to a man who was totally wrong for her.

Chance took her hand in his. ''You looked troubled for a second. Is something wrong?''

A bit of a smile, combined with a hint of

weariness, appeared when she unclenched her jaw. "No. I'm just a little tired, that's all."

He brought her hand to his mouth and brushed his lips lightly across her skin. "Before I leave…" He plumbed the depth of her eyes, wanting nothing more at that moment than to pull her body tightly against his and kiss away any concerns she might be harboring. "Would you go out with me tomorrow night? We could go to a movie or go dancing…or whatever you'd like to do."

"I—" She withdrew her hand from his grasp. His touch prevented her from thinking clearly, and she needed all her faculties to resist the threat he posed to what she believed was important—a stable home life where she could keep both feet planted firmly on solid ground. She rubbed her hand across the nape of her neck to still the shiver. "Thank you, but no. I don't think it would be a good idea."

"Why not?" He reclaimed her hand and pulled her close.

"We…we really don't have very much in common. We come from totally different backgrounds—"

"I think we have much more in common

than you think or know.'' He folded her in his arms, then covered her mouth with his.

His kiss was neither tentative nor subtle. Every bit of the heat that had existed before and had continued to simmer just beneath the surface instantly burst into flame. There was an excitement about him that surpassed all the truths she held so dear. As if her arms had a will of their own, she reached around his neck. Not only did she allow his kiss to continue, she fully returned one of her own.

Then reality intruded into the heated moment. This was the wrong thing to be doing and he was definitely the wrong man to be doing it with. Her arms slipped down until her hands rested against his tautly muscled chest. She felt his strong heartbeat as she stepped away and looked up into his eyes. What she saw was a dynamic man of many emotions and passions. A tremor rippled through her body. Fear or excitement? She was not sure she wanted to know.

Marcie tried to recover her composure while shoving back from Chance. At first he refused to release her from his embrace, then he reluctantly allowed her to step away. She quickly took another step backward, just enough to be out of his reach.

He saw her uncertainty and the wariness in her eyes. He also noted the kiss-swollen lushness of her mouth and the slight flush that highlighted her cheeks. He closed the distance between them, then ran his fingertips along her jawline and under her chin. "About tomorrow night? A movie? I'll pick you up at seven."

"No." Her voice quavered as she tried to bring some control to her words. "I, uh..." She shook her head. "No. I won't be able to go out with you tomorrow night." She edged toward the door, wanting nothing more at that moment than to get him out of her house and on his way before she lost her last remaining shred of resolve and caved in to his request.

"Thank you for dinner. I had a nice time." Her words were flat, her voice containing no emotion one way or the other.

"Yes, I can tell." A hint of despair slipped into his voice. "You won't go out with me tomorrow night and now you're doing your best to shove me out your door." He quickly covered it by flashing a sexy smile and surrounding his words with a teasing quality. "I'd hate to think what you'd do if you hadn't enjoyed yourself so much."

Chance had never before been in a spot like this. For the first time he felt a very real attraction to a special woman of substance who possessed so many qualities that had been missing in the type of women he usually dated. However, this very desirable woman had just flatly rejected him. And the qualities that he admired most, her independence and determination, were the same qualities that seemed to be causing his problems.

A strange sense of helplessness enveloped him and he did not know how to alleviate it. The situation was a unique one for him. There was no physical work he could do that would change the circumstances, and his fabled charm seemed to have failed him completely. Somehow he would have to solve the problem, but obviously it would not be tonight.

"Apparently it's time for me to leave." He tried not to sound too disappointed as he bid her good-night. "Thank you for joining me this evening. I know *I* certainly enjoyed it. Perhaps we can do it again sometime in the future." With that, Chance Fowler turned and left the house without looking back.

Marcie locked the door, turned out the light, then leaned back against the wall with her eyes closed. She had come within a breath of calling after him, inviting him to come back to build that fire in the fireplace. An uneasy self-reprimand settled inside her. She knew her behavior and attitude had been unacceptable, but it was the only way she could think of to distance herself from the spell he so effortlessly cast over her.

As she had done so many times during the past few days, she touched her fingers to her lips. Once again the heat of his kiss had seared through all her voiced objections and hidden concerns to strike at the core of her fears. Regardless of the circumstances surrounding his departure, she knew it would not be the end of Chance Fowler's presence in her life. She did not know whether that was cause to rejoice or to run and hide. It had been a long time since Marcie had felt this befuddled and she did not like the feeling.

She knew his type. Chance Fowler was a man who produced a disruptive affect on everything around him, then left chaos in his wake when he became bored and decided to move on to something new. Her personal en-

SHAWNA DELACORTE 85

counters with him had done nothing to change that opinion. Unfortunately that disruptive effect had worked its way into her normally calm and organized existence. He had literally turned her insides to mush, put a serious dent in her determination and left her without a clue as to what she could do about it other than hope it would go away.

Chance sat in his car in front of Marcie's house for a while, long enough to see the living room go dark and then one of the bedroom windows become illuminated. She had gotten under his skin and he knew he would not be able to ignore her. More importantly, he did not want to ignore her. He had to find some way to make sure that they had some reason to be together—perhaps some type of project that would keep them in contact.

He started his car. An idea began to swirl around in his head. He worked out the details as he drove home. The more he thought about it, the more the plan pleased him. It would satisfy two needs. It would provide a new project for his students, and it would also require her presence in his life, at least long enough for him to convince her he was not the headline-grabber the tabloid newspapers had painted him to be—a spoiled, rich playboy with no purpose in life or agenda for the future.

Four

———

Chance stared out the window as the jet touched down at San Francisco's airport. He had a meeting with Scott Blake of Blake Construction. Chance had purchased another fixer-upper house, this one in Oakland, as a project for his newest group of students. He exited the jetway and found Scott waiting for him. The two men shook hands as Scott greeted him.

"Chance, it's good to see you again. How was the flight?"

"Smooth and uneventful, just the way it should be." They walked along at a fast pace toward the exit. "How are Katherine and the children?"

They were soon headed north on the Bayshore Freeway toward the Oakland Bay Bridge. Half an hour later they pulled up in front of a two-story house built in the 1920s. They did a thorough walk-through with Chance showing Scott what he wanted done and Scott telling him how they could accomplish it. Then they sat down to work out a schedule for the remodeling project.

"I'd like to have this finished before Christmas, if that's possible. That only gives you a little over five weeks. Can you do it?"

Scott studied his notes for a moment. "I don't see any problem. The house is structurally sound and the roof was replaced five years ago. The kitchen is in pretty bad shape and the wiring needs to be redone, but most of the work is cosmetic."

Scott gave Chance a handwritten estimate of costs. "This is pretty close. I'll go over the figures in the morning and have an official quote faxed to you tomorrow afternoon. If it's acceptable, then we can get the contract out right away."

"That'll be fine. Did all my students report to you and fill out their paperwork?"

"Yes, everything's ready to go. We can get started on it as soon as the contract is signed."

They returned to Scott's car. "Will you be staying in town for a few days? Katherine would love to have you over to the house for dinner whatever night you're available."

"I'll have to take a rain check. I've got a flight in two hours. I need to be back in San Diego this evening. I have an appointment with my real estate broker. I've got him searching for another property. Hank Varney just finished up a remodeling project for me and I want to get started on another San Diego one as soon as possible."

A pensive look covered Scott's face for a moment, as if he were turning something over in his mind. Finally he spoke. "You know, Chance, you really should take advantage of all that media attention that follows you around and let people know about these trade schools you run. The press paints you with such a frivolous image. It's really not fair."

"No way. These kids have enough problems without every freelancer with a camera and the phone number of the local newspaper running around taking their pictures while they're trying to learn a trade and earn some money. They don't need their privacy invaded like that." It was something Chance felt very strongly about, and over the years he had steadfastly refused to budge on the matter.

Their immediate business concluded, Scott dropped Chance off at the airport and continued on his way. Chance boarded the next flight for San Diego and was soon home. As he drove from the airport to his house, his thoughts turned to Marcie Roper.

He had put his plan into the works early that morning before leaving for San Francisco. Hopefully his real estate broker had been able to find some properties for him to look at. If everything worked out the way he wanted, Marcie Roper would no longer be able to avoid him. He grabbed a quick bite to eat before his meeting.

Saturday found Marcie at the nursery, as usual. She had sent Chance Fowler from her house the previous Monday and had not heard from him since. She had busied herself during those days by pulling all of the Christmas merchandise together, but her heart and energy had not been with her work. She placed some of the items on display but held back on the others. The upcoming Thursday was Thanksgiving. She would put the rest of the Christmas items on display after the seasonal merchandise and specialty items for Thanksgiving had been removed.

Her nights, however, were a different matter. When she did not have work to occupy her mind, her thoughts unavoidably drifted toward Chance Fowler. But every time he entered her mind, she flashed on the image of the newspaper photograph showing the woman in the skimpy bikini hanging on his arm and looking up at him adoringly—just one of many, there was no doubt in her mind. And that image was followed by all the headlines she had ever seen that referred to him as a rich playboy and heir to a family fortune and business interests.

The first couple of days she told herself she was glad he had not called or tried to see her. Good riddance. Nothing viable could ever come from their continued association. But even as she tried to convince herself that he had made it easier for her by taking her hint and staying away, she knew it was not the case. Each passing day added to her sense of loss and strange sensation of abandonment. She did not understand any of it, but that did not make it any the less so.

She attempted to shake off the twinge of

melancholy that tried to force its way to the surface, rationalizing it as her normal Christmas blues. The only family she had was her father, and he was two thousand miles away in Illinois. Even though she had friends who always made it a point to include her in their holiday plans, it was still a lonely time for her. And now, as she looked around at the handmade Christmas ornaments and the festive wreaths on display, the loneliness deepened.

Then she thought of Chance and the moment of personal insight about his family that he had shared with her. Apparently his life was not all warm fuzzies, either. Perhaps he had been right when he'd said they had more in common than she realized.

In a moment of irritation she shoved away the ridiculous notion. They had absolutely nothing in common and that was the end of it. But if that was the case, then why did Chance Fowler constantly occupy her thoughts? Why had she reluctantly admitted to herself that she would not have minded seeing him again? Why did the mere thought of his kisses send a ripple of excitement through her body and make her yearn for much more?

And why did that realization frighten her right down to her toes?

She emitted a wistful sigh as she turned back to the reality of daily life. As soon as she put out the Open sign and unlocked the front door of the nursery, a steady stream of customers kept her busy. It was nearly closing time when she finally found a few moments to catch her breath and sit down.

"Marcie..." Glen stood at the back door. "Don and I are going to play basketball tonight. Would it be all right if we started closing up now so we can meet everyone at the high school gym at six-thirty?"

She offered a weary smile. "Sure, go ahead. I think the day-long rush of customers has finally come to an end." She rose from the bench. "In fact, why don't you take care of the cleanup and then leave? I'll lock up the back for you."

Glen flashed a grateful smile. "Thanks, Marcie. I'll see you in the morning." He hurried to the back lot to finish his chores.

Marcie took care of the end-of-day business, said good-night to Glen and Don, and locked the gate in the back fence and the truck delivery entrance. She was about to put the Closed sign in the window when she spotted Chance Fowler getting out of his car.

Her heart skipped a beat and she sucked in a sharp breath. She had not realized exactly how much she had missed him until that moment. The gentle ocean breeze ruffled his hair. The last fading rays of the sun highlighted his handsomely chiseled features. His stride was purposeful, conveying a very appealing confidence and sense of self that was neither cocky nor arrogant.

What woman in her right mind could possibly resist him, or would even want to, for that matter? The question did not bother her so much, but the answer most assuredly did. She tried her best to still the anxiety that told her she definitely fit into that category. She braced herself against the impending onslaught of a whirlwind named Chance Fowler and the havoc that resulted whenever he showed up.

The door opened and he stepped inside, filling the room with his dynamic presence. Marcie stood at the checkout counter and took a calming breath, but it did not help. Her insides melted the second he smiled at her.

"Did you miss me the past four days—five, counting today?"

She saw the teasing grin tug at the corners of his mouth and the prankish fun twinkle in the depths of his sky-blue eyes. As much as she wanted to be offended by his egotistical comment, she knew he had not intended it that way. She was determined, however, to maintain her distance from his mesmerizing allure.

"Oh? Has it been that long?" She adopted a standoffish attitude. "I assumed you had moved on to someone more suited to your shenanigans." The second the words were out of her mouth she regretted saying them. They sounded too harsh. What was there about this man that seemed to bring out the worst in her? Then she saw the edges of his eyes crinkle and a second later the entire room filled with the sound of his spontaneous laughter.

"*Shenanigans?* I haven't heard that word in ages. When I was a little boy my grandmother would use it whenever she caught me playing up in her attic. She would stand at the bottom of the stairs and call up to me. 'Chance, what kind of shenanigans are going on up there?'" His laugh changed to a warm smile. He seemed momentarily lost in fond remembrances.

The tender moment stirred a place of childhood memories for Marcie, too. An inner glow of pleasure worked its way to the surface in the form of a soft smile. "My grandmother used that word all the time. I guess you don't hear it much anymore."

He reached out and took her hand. His touch exuded a warmth that flooded her senses and radiated directly to her heart. It was a type of closeness she had not experienced in several years—not since her engagement. No, that had not been a valid assessment. She had *never* experienced that exact sensation with her ex-fiancé. Now she was more befuddled than ever.

He continued to clutch her hand as he led her around the corner of the counter, then pulled her into his embrace. "I had to make a quick trip to San Francisco on business, then had another business deal here that's taken all my time for the past few days." A teasing grin spread across his face as he continued to hold her. "I also wanted to give you enough time to realize that I'm not such a bad guy so that when I ask you out again you won't toss me out on my ear as your answer. You know, absence makes the heart grow fonder and all that."

He had not intended to put her on the spot, so he quickly changed the subject before she had an opportunity to respond. "Are you about through here?"

Being held in his embrace turned her determined resolve into pure bedlam. She had no idea what his game was, but she seemed doomed to be a participant. She felt herself being drawn in tighter and tighter. "I'm almost through. I let Glen and Don take off early, so I have the greenhouse and back storage areas to check and lock."

"I'll help you."

He had uttered the words with such tenderness that it sent a shiver of uncertainty through her body. She hesitated for a moment, then gave up all pretense to any objection.

"I—I need to lock the front door before we go out back."

A minute later he took her hand and they walked through the grounds to the back storage areas. She checked two large sheds and padlocked the doors. Then they went into the greenhouse where she did a walk-through, checking to make sure everything was in order while he waited by the door.

Chance watched her go through the procedures. He liked the way she moved, the sound of her voice, the feel of her skin, the taste of her kiss. And not just the physical, either. He liked her sense of self, her independence, her self-reliance, her intelligence. He liked everything he knew about her. And he wanted to know so much more.

It took Marcie about ten minutes to get everything taken care of in the greenhouse. She returned to where he waited by the door. "That's it. Nothing left to do but lock the greenhouse door, turn on the security lights, set the alarm, then leave through the front."

"Well, maybe there's one more thing that needs to be done."

He pulled her into his arms and covered her mouth with his. After only a moment's hesitation she slipped her arms around his neck and responded fully. His kiss spoke of tenderness underscored by a heated passion—a very provocative and addictive combination. And she suspected that she just might be well on her way to becoming hopelessly addicted.

He felt something jab him in the back when he leaned against the wall, but he dismissed it as totally unimportant. He pulled her body closer, snuggling her hips against his. He nibbled at the corners of her mouth, then slipped his tongue between her lips. The flame building between them pumped up the heat by several degrees.

Without warning, the sprinkler heads sputtered. Then the water shot out with full force, soaking everything—plants and people alike. The sudden intrusion of cold water startled them to attention, but not to the point where Chance released her from his embrace. He tried to suppress a grin, but his efforts were to no avail. His smile widened, then turned into a full-blown laugh. A second later her involuntary laugh burst forth and joined his in a wonderfully free moment of childlike fun.

"I have to admit that it was getting warm in here, but I didn't think it was hot enough to set off the sprinkler system." His laugh died and the smile faded from his face. He held her gaze with his as surely as he held her body cradled in his arms. His voice took on a bit of a husky quality. "At least, not yet."

Chance continued to hold her as the cold spray cascaded over them, soaking their clothes and plastering their hair against their heads. Neither of them made any attempt to reach for the switch Chance had activated when he'd leaned against the wall. Neither made any attempt to get away from the drenching shower.

Rivulets of water ran down her face and matted her eyelashes into spiky clumps. He brushed the water from her cheeks, leaving a damp sheen. Droplets clung to her lips. He felt the tightness pull across his chest and the heat settle low inside him.

"I'm sure you've heard this many times, but it's worth repeating." His words were barely above a whisper. "You're a very beautiful woman, Marcie Roper. Very desirable, very—" He quickly recaptured her mouth, leaving the rest of his thoughts unspoken.

She returned the passion of his kiss as they each ignored the steady shower of water coming from the sprinklers.

Chance opened the door to Marcie's bathroom and stepped out into the hallway. He had put on the sweatpants and clean pair of socks he kept in the trunk of his car and had the sweatshirt slung over his shoulder. He met Marcie as she came out of her bedroom where she had changed into jeans and a sweater. He handed her his wet clothes and she put them in the dryer along with hers.

She returned to the living room a few minutes later, carrying two glasses of wine. She paused in the doorway and watched him as he towel dried his hair. He had tossed his sweatshirt over the arm of the sofa. Her gaze drifted across his muscular chest, broad shoulders and strong arms, and lingered on the way his sweatpants rested low on his hips. He was most definitely a prime physical specimen.

She closed her eyes and took in a deep breath to calm the heated excitement that churned inside her. She took a second breath, but it did not help. When she opened her eyes she discovered, much to her relief, that he had pulled on his sweatshirt.

She entered the living room. "Here." She held out one of the glasses toward him. "Maybe this will help take off the chill."

He took the glass from her and extended a warm smile. "Thanks." He took a sip of the wine, then set the glass on the fireplace mantel. "If it's okay with you, I thought I'd bring in some wood and build a fire. That should help take off the chill, too."

As much as she feared what could happen

if he did stay, it was nothing compared to how much she did not want him to leave. She had sent him from her house once before, but she knew she would not be doing it again. She stared up into his eyes. Her breath caught in her throat before she totally succumbed to the overwhelming power of his magnetic pull. She returned his smile. "That would be very nice."

Chance soon had a cozy fire going. He closed the fireplace screen, then took Marcie's hand and led her to the sofa. He leaned back into the corner, pulling her down next to him. She willingly snuggled into the comfort of his arms. Silence seemed to come quite naturally to them. Neither felt pressured to carry on a conversation. There was no awkwardness in the quiet.

They watched the flames dance across the logs, listened to the popping and crackling of the burning wood, and basked in the golden glow. Her head rested against his shoulder. A soft feeling of intimacy settled over the room. Each seemed to be lost in the privacy of personal thoughts.

Chance pulled her body over on top of his as he stretched out on the sofa. He wrapped her in the warmth of his embrace. Every few minutes he brushed his lips against her forehead or cheek. As the minutes ticked away, those innocent little kisses became more and more frequent until the two of them were fully involved in a sensually delicious kiss of the type that could only lead to far more intimate activities.

He captured her mouth with an increased fervor—twining his tongue with hers, relishing the texture and devouring her taste. He felt her firm breasts press against his chest as he held her in his arms; each breath she drew added to the sexual heat of the moment. He slipped his hand under her sweater and trailed his fingers across her back. Her smooth skin provided a tactile sensation that filled him with a need for much more.

Marcie met every one of his heated advances with a response of equal intensity. She ran her fingers through his thick hair before circling her arms around his neck. She felt his breathing, the solid rhythm of his strong heartbeat.

Neither Chance nor Marcie could deny the energy that sizzled between them, but it was more than merely the desires of physical passion. There was a very deep emotional connection trying to take hold. It created a seductively intimate mood—for Chance, perhaps a bit too comfortable; for Marcie, frighteningly real.

She knew he was the wrong man for her. No matter how much he fueled her desires he would never be the solid, dependable type of man she had been searching for. The type of man she needed in her life. Someone capable of making a lifelong commitment and sticking with it. Someone who could be happy with a stable home, a family, and content with the life-style that went with it.

She reluctantly, and with considerable difficulty, broke off the kiss and pulled back from him. She tried to calm her ragged breathing before saying anything. "This...this is too much, too fast. I hardly know you."

He looked into the depth of her eyes, into the honesty that could not be hidden—an honesty that clearly revealed her vulnerability. He traced the outline of her kiss-swollen lips with his fingertip. His voice held a husky quality that he could not control. "I thought we were getting to know each other pretty well." He did not know what else to say. Anything other than that would have revealed too much of what was going on inside him, and he could not risk that.

She pushed back from him a little more. "Yes, a little *too* well." A hint of trepidation covered her words.

The next thing he knew she had scrambled to her feet. He had been correct when he decided Marcie Roper was not the type of woman who would carry on a casual affair or who would be willing to play games. The growing realization that told him this was not a game he was playing had a very disturbing effect on him.

He drained the last swallow of wine from his glass, then rose to his feet, put his arm around her shoulder and walked with her to the kitchen. He pulled her into his embrace and placed a gentle kiss on her forehead. He did not want to leave, but knew he was risking too much if he stayed. It was the most expedient thing to do under the circumstances.

"Do you suppose my clothes are dry yet?" His question lacked any and all enthusiasm.

"Yes, I'm sure they are." Her answer did not hold any more pleasure at the prospect of his leaving than his question had. She was very thankful that he had taken matters into his hands and made the decision to leave. She turned to get his clothes from the dryer, but did not get very far.

Chance caught her arm and pulled her back into his embrace. Good intentions be damned. If she wanted him to leave, then she would have to say so. He recaptured her mouth with an intensity that left nothing to the imagination.

Marcie finally broke off the kiss. Her words were tentative, echoing the uncertainty that jittered inside her. ''I—I think you'd better leave before...'' Her voice dropped to a mere whisper as she searched for the proper thing to say. She stared at the floor, embarrassment over the nature of the conversation taking hold of her senses. ''Before things get completely out of hand.''

He placed his fingertips beneath her chin and lifted her face until he could look into her eyes. ''And would it be so terrible if they did?''

Five

_____

"Hey, Marcie—"

She jumped at the sound of her name and whirled around to see Glen standing in the door of the greenhouse. Even though it was Sunday, she had come in to start on an inventory list her insurance company needed.

"Sorry, Marcie. I didn't mean to scare you." He eyed her suspiciously. "You seem a little frazzled. Are you okay?"

She forced a smile. "Sure. You just startled me, that's all. I didn't hear you come in. What do you need?"

"There's some guy at the front counter asking for you. His name's Chance Fowler. He says it's a business matter."

Her brow wrinkled into a slight frown. ''A business matter? Did he say what it was?''

''Nope, just asked for you.'' Having delivered the message, Glen turned and left the greenhouse, leaving a perplexed Marcie staring after him.

There was no way she would have heard Glen come up behind her. Her mind was a million miles away and totally absorbed with thoughts of the very same Chance Fowler and where the previous evening might have gone— *could easily* have gone—if she had not asked him to leave. She could tell when he walked out her front door that he had not wanted to leave any more than she'd wanted him to, but she knew it was the only way. He was wrong for her...wrong, wrong, wrong. And no matter how many passion-filled kisses they shared, that fact could not be changed.

She had spent a lousy night tossing and turning until sunrise finally forced her out of bed. And now the reason for her sleepless night had once again presented himself at her place of business without warning. A little sigh of despondency escaped her lips as she walked toward the front of the nursery. She wished she could muster the fortitude to tell him she did not want to see him anymore. She also wished she could convince herself that she really meant it—that each time she heard his voice her heart did not skip a beat, that her insides did not turn to a mass of quivering jelly every time his lips touched hers.

Chance paced up and down in front of the counter as he waited for Marcie. The unaccustomed nervousness that had plagued him from the instant he climbed out of bed that morning left him edgy and uncomfortable. He had never before gone to such lengths to be with a woman, especially one who continued to offer more rejection than encouragement. But then, he had never met a woman who was worth all the extra effort. He knew beyond a doubt that Marcie Roper was definitely that very special woman. He had carefully worked out his plan and was now ready to present it. He swallowed down his anxiety as he watched her enter through the back door.

He forced a confident smile. "Hello. I went to your house, but you weren't there. Even though it's Sunday, I thought you might be here, so I stopped by to see." He chuckled nervously. "And here you are."

She returned his smile with a somewhat tentative one of her own. "Yes, here I am. I'm doing inventory. Glen said you had some business you wanted to discuss."

"Yes." He nervously cleared his throat. "I've purchased a fixer-upper cottage a few blocks from here and I'd like to hire your company to do the landscaping. I'm afraid it needs everything. Right now the yard consists of a few weeds and a lot of dirt."

"Landscaping? That's the business you wanted to discuss?" A feeling of relief settled over her. A straightforward business deal, nothing personal and certainly no intimate contact.

As if in defiance of her thoughts, he reached across the counter and grasped her hand in his. "Could I get you to ride along with me and look the place over? That way you can give me an estimate of cost so that I can figure it in with the remodeling expenses."

She glanced at her watch, then out the front window. "I'm afraid it's going to be dark before I can get away from here. How about tomorrow sometime?" She reached beneath the counter and brought out an estimate pad.

He squeezed her hand and flashed a warm

smile. "Tomorrow it is. I'll pick you up at ten o'clock in the morning."

An amused chuckle escaped her throat. "You're getting ahead of things. Before that, I need to get some information." She picked up a pen. "Client name...Chance Fowler. Phone number..." She looked up at him. She had assumed that he did not have an ordinary nine-to-five job, but it suddenly occurred to her that she did not have a clue as to where he lived, how to get in touch with him, what he did with his time every day. His mere presence sent her normally sensible and logical nature into a tailspin, yet she did not know a thing about the man behind the headlines. And she wanted to know everything.

He took the pen from her. "Why don't I fill this out for you?" He provided the information required and returned the form to her.

She took a moment to look it over before continuing. "What type of a budget do you have for this?"

"I haven't figured one. Whatever it costs."

"Well, you'll have to give me some kind of an idea of what you want to spend, what type of landscaping we'll be doing. Do you want a low-maintenance yard—just the lawn, some trees and easy-care shrubbery, or are we talking elaborate plantings? Will there be a gardener to maintain things after we've completed the work?''

''Why don't we discuss this in the morning after you've looked the place over? Meanwhile, tonight...'' He brought her hand to his lips and brushed a soft kiss across her palm.

That was all it took. Marcie Roper, the levelheaded business person and sensible woman, melted under the warmth of his touch just as she imagined so many other women had done. She could barely get out the words as her voice turned to an almost inaudible whisper. ''Tonight? What about tonight?''

''We'll go to the movie we missed last night.'' An impish grin tugged at the corners of his mouth. ''Unless you'd rather tackle the sprinkler system in the greenhouse again.'' He ran his fingertips across her cheek, cupped her chin in his hand, then leaned across the counter and placed a tender kiss on her lips. ''I'll pick you up at your house at seven-thirty.''

She simply nodded her head in agreement, unable to force out any words. She felt totally helpless, as if she were completely under the spell of this dynamic, sexy and very tempting

man with whom she had nothing in common—
nothing except the fact that his touch made her
insides melt and her heart race totally out of
control.

He gave her hand one last squeeze, then left
the nursery. She watched him walk across the
parking lot and get in his car. What had she
gotten herself into? And how could she get
herself out of it? Perhaps the more important
question was whether or not she really wanted
to get herself out of it.

It was a question she chose not to answer
as she returned to the greenhouse to continue
her inventory. It was also a question that remained very close to the forefront of her consciousness as she completed her day's work
and prepared to leave.

She hurried home, changed clothes, and was
running a brush through her hair just as
Chance rang her doorbell. Still a little flustered
from her rush to be ready by seven-thirty, she
opened the door and let him in.

"Hi." He placed a quick kiss on her cheek
as he entered her living room. "Are you ready
to go?"

"Just barely. I only got home about fifteen

minutes ago. What movie are we going to see?''

''Whatever you want to see. Do you have a newspaper? We'll check what's playing.''

She grabbed the morning paper and turned to the entertainment section. They scanned the movie listings and agreed on a comedy.

As they walked to his car he put his arm around her shoulder. ''You said you just got home? Have you had any dinner? We can stop and get something to eat and then catch a later showing.''

Everything about it felt so comfortable and natural. Her bouts with anxiety and uncertainty seemed to have been shoved into the background. Could it have been something as simple as him wanting to hire her company for a business matter? In that one little conversation he had let her know he respected her and her abilities.

They decided to go to the movie first. Afterward they picked up a pizza and took it back to Marcie's house. Thoughts of food did not last very long, though. Only two slices of pizza had been consumed and the rest of it remained in the box on the kitchen counter. Two half-full glasses of wine sat on the coffee table in the living room.

Chance and Marcie reclined against the large floor pillows in front of the fireplace. He held her in his embrace, each seemingly lost in the dancing flames that radiated a special warmth through the room. The popping and crackling of the burning wood only added to the sensual atmosphere.

It all started innocently enough. Chance placed a tender kiss on her forehead and Marcie responded by snuggling closer against him. He nuzzled her neck, then kissed her cheek. It may not have been a purposeful seduction, but it did not take long for one kiss to lead to another as he held her body pressed tightly against his. And with each kiss came an increased level of passion.

Chance caressed her shoulders and back. Odd thoughts, totally out of character, floated through his mind. He was concerned about rushing her, about making her feel uncomfortable. It was far removed from the thoughts and feelings that usually ran rampant when he was with a desirable woman—thoughts and feelings controlled by his libido. This was so different. Things seemed to come from a different place this time—a place of caring and respect.

She felt so good in his arms. He twined his tongue with hers, the texture stimulating his senses and telling him he wanted much more. He wanted her taste, the feel of her skin, the excitement she stirred deep inside him. He wanted all of her—body and soul.

Marcie felt herself slipping further and further under the charismatic spell of Chance Fowler. She had never met anyone like him. He made her feel things she had never felt before. She teetered on the edge of totally giving herself over to the passions churning inside her. Unfortunately her desires also perched her on the brink of her own internal conflict. She wanted him. She wanted what he made her feel. And it frightened her. He was as wrong for her as could be, yet she did not know how to cool her fervor.

Each heated moment escalated their personal feelings and brought them closer to the realization of exactly how much was at stake on an emotional level. Putting a stop to things before they went too far was even more difficult than last time, but it was something they both knew needed to be done before it was too late.

Marcie broke the kiss just long enough to gasp, "I—I think this has maybe gone too far."

His voice was a husky whisper and disbelief surrounded his words. "What? You...what?"

She managed to get into a sitting position while disentangling herself from his arms. "I..." She tried to smooth her hair back in an attempt to stall for time as she collected her composure. "I think it would be wise to allow cooler heads to prevail."

"Perhaps you're right." His disappointment was obvious as he rose to his feet. "I'll see you tomorrow morning." He gave her one last look of longing, then headed for the door.

Chance parked his car at the curb, then gestured toward the cottage. "Here it is. As I said, it's a fixer-upper, but it should look pretty good when we finish the renovations." He got out and quickly walked around to the passenger side to open the door for Marcie.

She slid out of the seat and looked around. A construction company truck and three other cars were parked at the house, even though no one was in sight. The yard was exactly what he had said it was, a few weeds and lots of dirt. The house was a lot larger than she had anticipated. His use of the word "cottage" had made her think of something much smaller than this two-story house with the wraparound porch, sitting on what appeared to be a third of an acre of land.

He guided her up the front walk. "Come on. I'll show you around the inside, then we can discuss the yard."

As Marcie stepped up on the porch with Chance, a stocky man in his fifties walked out the front door. He flashed Marcie a warm smile.

Chance quickly made introductions. "Hank, this is Marcie Roper of Crestview Bay Landscaping. Her company will be doing the grounds. Marcie, this is Hank Varney. He's the contractor. I imagine the two of you will be running into each other several times over the next few weeks."

Marcie and Hank shook hands. "It's a pleasure to meet you, Marcie. If you need anything, give me a shout."

Hank turned his attention to Chance. "I've got Jim, Bob, and Fred working inside. I had planned to put Jeff on whatever your next project turned out to be, but…well, I guess I need to replace him. Do you have someone—''

Chance quickly cut off Hank's conversation. ''Let's discuss this later. I'll give you a call this afternoon after Marcie and I finish going over the landscaping needs.''

Marcie caught Chance's quick effort to keep Hank from finishing his sentence. It was obvious that there was something she was not supposed to hear. And what had Hank meant by his ''next project''? Was the remodeling of this old house something more than met the eye? Too many questions and no answers.

Chance Fowler was becoming more complex with each new encounter. That pleased her very much. She hated the idea that she had fallen for someone with no more depth than what the newspaper stories presented. A little scowl momentarily furrowed her forehead as she recalled the photograph taken after the sailboat regatta with the woman clinging to his arm and looking up at him adoringly. It seemed to her that the unnamed woman would be more in tune with Chance Fowler's lifestyle, and the notion saddened her. She had hoped that perhaps she might be the one.

She swallowed hard as the full impact of her uncensored thoughts hit her reality. Had she truly fallen for this disconcerting man beyond the undeniable intense physical attraction she felt toward him? Was there more going on than merely the physical pull? And what about Chance? Exactly where did Chance Fowler think any of this was headed? Was it nothing more for him than just a game?

Chance placed his hand at the small of her back, jarring her out of her thoughts. He gently guided her toward the door. "Come on, I'll show you around." As soon as they stepped inside she heard the sounds of hammering and sawing coming from the second floor where people were obviously hard at work.

They started with the entry hall. "As you can see, this house has obviously been neglected over the years, but it shows lots of promise. The foundation is solid, as is the overall structure. We're primarily looking at cosmetic problems."

He took her into the large living room. "Under this mess of old paint—" he pointed out window trim, moldings, doors, and the banister and staircase "—is beautiful solid oak. I can't imagine why someone would want to paint over it.'' He turned to face her, as if something had just occurred to him. ''Do you know that we actually found six layers of paint on this gorgeous staircase? In six different colors?'' He ran his fingers across one of the balusters supporting the handrail. ''Look at the carving on this. When the renovations are finished, it will once again be beautiful polished oak.''

He ushered her across the living room. ''It's the same with this fireplace mantel. It's made of hand-carved oak, but it's been hidden for years underneath all these layers of ugly paint.''

He took her completely through the house, explaining what he planned to do in each and every room. They finally stepped out into the backyard. ''I've told you everything I plan to do inside. Now, what do you think about the yard?''

Marcie shook her head in amazement. This was a far cry from what she had anticipated. ''You'll have to let me catch my breath. You pretty much overwhelmed me with all your plans.'' It was more than his remodeling plans that had her overwhelmed. Her sensibilities reeled from the whirlwind dose of an energetic Chance Fowler involved in something he obviously loved. He was like a nonstop dynamo set to full-speed-ahead. She was having a very difficult time reconciling the man she had just seen and heard with the same man the newspapers had painted as a shallow playboy.

"Well? What do you think?" The enthusiasm beamed from his face much like a little boy with a new toy.

"You seem to know quite a lot about renovating old houses."

"Yeah, I guess so." He looked away from her, staring off toward the horizon as if lost in thought. His response became more vague. "I guess you could say it's something I dabble in from time to time."

He wanted to share his excitement about the project with her. He liked the sound of it and the idea of it—the two of them sharing, working together...being together. His mind jumped at the idea of her doing all the landscaping for all his house renovation projects. He liked it very much.

The moment was a quiet, reflective one for each of them. It seemed to her as if it were a time that should be shared. In some ways she felt so open and comfortable with him, but in other ways she felt awkward. When she thought of *his world*—who he was, the people he knew, the places he went—it only served to remind her of how much their worlds differed. Would it ever be possible for him to want the same things out of life as she did?

She was not sure why, but she had an almost irresistible urge to reach out and take his hand even though she knew it would be unwise. Before she had time to give it any more thought, he took the decision away from her.

He grasped her hand in his and together they stepped off the back porch and out into the yard. "I've given you the rundown on what's going to happen with the house, so suppose you give me a rough idea of what I should do with this pile of dirt and weeds?"

"Well, that brings me back to yesterday's question. Do you want a basic low-maintenance yard that will be easy to take care of, or something more elaborate that will require a gardener or at the very least, someone living in the house who really enjoys working in the yard? Maybe it would help if I knew what you planned to do with the house when you're finished with the renovations."

"My plan is to sell it."

"Then I'd suggest something in between the

two extremes.'' She took an art pad from her shoulder bag and began sketching the layout of the area within the fence, including the exterior of the house. ''We can definitely enhance the appearance of the property from the street, making it a more attractive package without blowing out your budget. We can also use the landscaping to give additional privacy without creating a potentially dangerous situation of providing trespassers someplace to hide and thereby compromising security.''

''It sounds perfect. I also want you to add in an underground sprinkler system in the front and back. Give me something to sign and I'll have a check to you immediately. Now, how about lunch?''

''Just like that? You don't want to see a rendering first, along with a quote so that you can get other bids before making a decision?''

''Nope. I'm sure your price will be fair and the finished job will look terrific.'' He flashed her a confident smile as he grabbed her hand again. ''You can finish that sketch some other time. Right now, let's go to lunch.''

''I'm afraid that won't be possible. I have too much work to do and can't spare the time." She glanced at her watch. "In fact, I need to get back to the nursery right away."

They returned to his car and he drove her back to work. He pulled up in front of the nursery door. "Okay, you're off the hook for lunch." He brushed an errant lock of hair away from her cheek, then allowed his fingers to linger against her skin. His voice dropped to a seductive timbre. "What about tonight?"

She suddenly felt as if all the oxygen had been pulled from her lungs as a herd of unruly butterflies stampeded through her stomach. She knew his kiss and the very disconcerting effect it had on her; his touch grabbed her in much the same way. She fought to control her voice so that it sounded calm and natural rather than breathless and uncertain. She avoided eye contact with him, knowing that was all it would take to pull her effortlessly into the heady realm of his tantalizing sex appeal. She nervously cleared her throat. "I already have plans for tonight...it's, uh, a business meeting."

It was the truth, as far as it went. Her meeting was with Glen and Eric Ross, who ran the landscaping crew, for the purpose of discussing new business. She would add Chance's project to the list of upcoming jobs. Of course, the meeting could have easily been moved to another evening—a thought that had tickled across her mind before she dismissed it. She still had reservations about their personal involvement in spite of the very real attraction she felt for him. The previous night's passionate interlude had gone a long way toward telling her just how much she was already emotionally involved with him and it frightened her.

"Maybe if your meeting doesn't run too late—"

Even though he did not finish what he had started to say, she saw the question in his eyes and sensed the warmth in his voice. She felt her determination begin to melt away. She quickly opened the car door and slid out before he could initiate any more physical contact between them.

"I'll have a quote for you in a couple of days on the landscaping project, along with drawings showing how it will be laid out when it's completed. Will that be soon enough?"

He could not hide his disappointment. "Sure, that will be fine." It was obvious that he would not be seeing her that night. He watched as she entered the nursery, then disappeared into the back room.

He pulled out of the parking lot and headed toward home. His thoughts were filled with exactly where the previous night's passion might have taken them if Marcie had not put a stop to things. As disappointed as he was, he knew she was right. He did not want to make any mistakes with her. He wanted to make sure their relationship was on solid footing before taking it to the next level.

A little twinge of anxiety pricked at his senses. He had used the word "relationship." It was a word that did not fit comfortably with him. Relationship was the road that led to commitment...no detours, no exits. It was a road he had purposely and consistently chosen not to travel. There had always been too many other roads that led to all types of interesting places and adventures and he had been happy with them. But now he found himself on the road of relationship on his way to commitment. Perhaps things had already gone too far.

Marcie parked in the driveway behind Hank Varney's truck. It was barely daylight. She was surprised that the construction people were working so early in the morning. She grabbed her sketch pad. She needed to do an accurate sketch of the house and property and take some measurements so she could go back to her office and work out a landscaping proposal for Chance.

She felt at a bit of a loss and more than a little irritated with him for simply dumping the entire thing in her lap without any guidelines. He had left everything up to her without a budget or even a mention of any personal likes and dislikes for her to take under consideration. She was not sure exactly where to begin.

She did not want him to think she was purposely overdoing things to increase her profit. On the other hand, she did not want him to be disappointed because he had expected more from her than what she had delivered. Maybe she could get some insight from Hank Varney.

She wandered around inside the house for a few minutes, taking special notice of the little details he had pointed out—things she knew she would not have noticed on her own. He had opened her eyes to the charm and beauty of the house hidden beneath layers of paint and years of neglect. It had been an insightful look into the way he saw things. He made an effort to dig beneath the surface to find the treasures that had been hidden from view—certainly not the actions of a shallow self-centered playboy.

"Good morning, Marcie." Hank stood in the doorway between the living room and dining room. "I'm surprised to see you here so early. Is there something I can help you with?"

"Good morning. I just wanted to do some sketches and get some measurements so I can plan out the landscaping."

He turned to leave. "If you need anything, give me a shout."

"There is something…"

He paused for a moment. "Yes?"

"Well…" She joined him at the doorway, not wanting to carry on a conversation from across the room and take a chance on the other workers hearing her. "I'm afraid this is a little awkward." She tried to properly formulate her words without having them sound as if she were prying. "It's just that Chance wouldn't give me any kind of a budget or tell me what he had in mind. He left all the decisions to me, but I'm not sure what he wants."

She took out her notebook and pencil. "You've worked for him before, haven't you?"

"Sure, I've done all of Chance's San Diego school projects same way that Scott Blake does all of his San Francisco school projects."

Had she heard him correctly? *School* projects? She spoke hesitantly, not sure where the conversation was headed. "I'm afraid I don't understand. I thought this was just a house he bought to fix up and sell at a profit and he hired your company to do the renovations for him. What do you mean by *school* projects?"

Hank nervously shifted his weight from one foot to the other. "I shouldn't have said that. I guess I assumed your being here meant you knew about Chance's projects."

"Would you tell me about them?" She tried to convey all the sincerity and genuine interest that was inside her rather than having it appear as nothing more than idle curiosity. "I'd really like to know. I'm having a devil of a time trying to figure him out. He seems to be a true enigma. Maybe this will help."

Hank furrowed his brow for a moment, obviously giving careful consideration to her question. "Well...I guess it wouldn't hurt anything now. Don't imagine Chance would have hired you to do the landscaping if he didn't trust you."

Trust. It had never occurred to her that someone would not trust her. She was an honest person. But now that Hank had brought it up, she realized that it would probably be difficult for someone in Chance's position to really trust strangers. He would need to build that trust over time while constantly being on his guard against people trying to take advantage of his financial position or family name. A warm feeling of contentment settled over her. Chance Fowler had chosen to place his trust in her.

Hank motioned for her to walk with him as he went up the stairs to the second floor. ''For several years now Chance has underwritten a training program for disadvantaged kids, primarily older teens of eighteen or nineteen who dropped out of school for one reason or another and are now having a rough time of it. He buys a house and then the kids do the work, under my supervision and with the occasional help of some of my regular construction crew.

''Instead of the students having to pay to go to school to learn a trade, Chance pays them a wage while they're training. When the project is finished he sells the house and buys another one. When his students have been sufficiently trained, we work them into full-time jobs. All the profits from the sale go back into the next project.''

''I had no idea...'' A sense of awe tinged her whispered response to what Hank had told her. An unexpected feeling of pride seeped through her consciousness as she realized just how special Chance Fowler was and what a privilege it was to be associated with one of his projects. The Chance Fowler she had just learned about was far removed from the man gracing the tabloid headlines who had grabbed her on the street and kissed her senseless. This was a man truly worth knowing.

''Not many people do. Chance likes to maintain a real low profile on his association with the schools.''

''You keep using the word 'school.' Is this something that's sanctioned by the state or the board of education?''

''Not exactly. Chance works with some municipal and state agencies, but mostly it's just Chance doing his bit to help out some young people who would otherwise probably end up in jail and not have an opportunity to make something of their lives. He's very careful to make sure no one associates him with any of this. He's always afraid that one of the tabloids will get hold of the story and blow it up on their front page. The last thing he wants is for any of these kids to be held up to public scrutiny because of who he is.''

''You mean, this isn't even a legal business?''

''It's legal, all right. Chance has it registered as a nonprofit organization. There has to be some way of accounting for the money and that seemed to be the best way, especially since Chance doesn't take a penny's worth of profits from it.''

''It sounds as if you've known him for a long time. His family must be very proud of his dedication.'' She was not sure why she had said that. She already knew that Chance and his father did not get along. But surely this would be different. This was something that should transcend a mere personality conflict.

Hank could not hold back the disdainful laugh. ''Yeah. I've known Chance for a lot of years. I used to work for Douglas Fowler. Chance went to him with his idea about the schools and his old man told him it was a waste of money and he didn't want the Fowler name associated with it.''

Hank struck a pose, his lowered voice taking on a sarcastic tone. "'The Fowler name means profit, not nonprofit. I don't want to hear any more about this stupidity.'" He took in a deep breath, held it for a moment, then expelled it. "Anyway, that's what the old man told him. That was several years ago and Chance wasn't even asking for something for himself." His voice took on a hint of sadness. "That was the moment Chance cut his father out of his life. He has never asked his father for anything since that day nor has he accepted anything his father has offered. They're more like strangers than father and son. I blame the old man for it, not Chance."

"I knew he didn't get along with his father, but I didn't realize they were truly estranged. You mean, they don't speak to each other at all?" She recalled Chance holding up the computer printout of the e-mail announcing his father's marriage.

"They maintain contact, but it's usually strained and impersonal. Chance's compassion, caring, and sense of social responsibility are a result of his mother's influence. There's always the obligatory holiday season get-together and with Christmas approaching he's

probably getting a little tense about the prospect.''

''Well...I guess I'd better...'' Marcie held
up her notebook, gestured toward the stairs,
and extended a weak smile before going back
to the first floor. Any and all words failed her
as she made her way down the stairs. Her mind
worked feverishly to assimilate all the information Hank had given her—starting with
what he had said about Chance trusting her.

A soft warmth started as a little spot in the
pit of her stomach and quickly spread throughout her body. Suddenly everything about
Chance Fowler seemed so very right. But that
spot of warmth was short-lived. A moment
later reality set back in.

Perhaps there was this side of him that not
many people knew about, but that did not ne-
gate his very real playboy life-style—something she knew to be true from firsthand
knowledge. After all, it was that brash playboy
she had first encountered on the street. Nor did
it change the fact that he could never be the
type of man she wanted to spend the rest of
her life with no matter how much she was attracted to him.

Six

Marcie looked over the final plans for the landscaping. She had two drawings, one showing the front yard as seen from the street and the other showing the backyard. She had put most of the effort into the front yard, making sure the grounds looked good from the street to enhance the sales prospects. She had left the back as primarily lawn with some plantings around the edge of the yard. It was a large yard and it had occurred to her that whoever bought the house might want to put in a swimming pool or even a tennis court.

She was very pleased with the work she had done. She hoped Chance would also like it. She printed out the detailed quote from her computer and also a letter of agreement for him to sign.

It had been two days since she had seen him. He had not called or stopped by, even to check on how she was doing with his bid. She had given considerable thought to what Hank Varney had told her about Chance. It seemed like a long time ago when she had first spotted him running down the street toward her. He had bothered her with his continued unwelcome attentions. And now, two days without seeing him felt like an eternity. As much as she did not want it to be so, she was totally involved and there was no use in her trying to rationalize it as being anything other than what she knew it was—she was absolutely crazy about Chance Fowler.

She should have been happy, but instead she felt uncertain and confused. Just because she was falling for him did not mean that he felt the same way about her. She still worried that for Chance Fowler this might be just another of his games—pleasant diversion for the time being but not anything lasting. It was one more thing to add to her seasonal blues.

Her thoughts were interrupted by a customer. She rang up an advance order for a large holiday wreath for the front door, four poinsettia plants, some holly sprigs, and one hundred feet of evergreen garland to decorate the banister of a staircase and the railing along a loft overlooking an entry hall. She sighed audibly as she watched the customer drive away. She knew she needed to start decorating her own house, even if for no other reason than the annual employee Christmas party. The next day was Thanksgiving and the nursery would be closed. Maybe she could get to it then.

Business remained steady for the rest of the day. She finally put out the Closed sign, locked the front door, and began the end-of-day closing procedures. She looked up at the sound of someone tapping at the front window. She immediately spotted Chance standing there, grinning at her. She could not have stopped the big smile from spreading across her face even if she had wanted to. She hurried to let him in.

He pulled her into his arms. ''I wasn't happy with the answer I got last time I asked you this question. Hopefully this time you'll do better.'' He brushed a soft kiss across her lips. ''Have you missed me the past couple of days?'' His teasing grin was in place, but his eyes showed a depth of sincere feeling that went far beyond his words.

A shortness of breath caught her by surprise. She tried to stop the quivering sensation that had attacked her insides the moment he touched her. She forced a calm to her voice, but knew the attempt was futile. "I suppose I missed you a little bit."

His face was so close to hers he could almost feel her words as she spoke. Her breasts pressed against his chest with each breath she took. His voice came out huskier than he wanted. "Only a little bit?"

Before she could answer, he lowered his mouth to hers. At that precise moment nothing else mattered to him. He held her body tightly against his and ran his fingers through the silky strands of her hair. The earthy response of her kiss filled him with a special type of sensual excitement that he had not experienced in a long time—if ever. It was an irresistible mixture of warmth, caring, closeness…and against his conscious desire, perhaps the beginnings of love.

He finally broke off the kiss, but he didn't release her from his embrace. "Are you about through here?"

"Give me five minutes and I will be."

"Do you have any plans for tonight?"

Her words came out in a breathless whisper. "No...none."

"What about tomorrow, for Thanksgiving? Any plans that would prevent us from going sailing?"

Again her answer was more of a hushed breath than actual words. "No, no plans at all."

Marcie quickly finished her chores and locked up. Chance grasped her hand in his and led her to his car.

"Where are we going? Could we drop my car at my house first?"

"Sure. I'll follow you home."

Before long they were headed south out of Crestview Bay. They continued on to San Diego, across the bridge to Coronado Island and finally arrived at Chance's house, located on a quiet, tree-lined side street.

Marcie stepped through the front door of the old Spanish-style house with its red-tiled roof and graceful arches. It was not at all what she had expected. The house was smaller than she thought it would be. It was very attractive and tastefully decorated, but it did not reek of big money and status. It exuded a personal warmth that she found very comfortable and quite appealing. She did notice that it was as devoid of holiday decor as her own house.

"This is really lovely, Chance."

"Thank you. I'm glad you like it." He escorted her through the living room. "Let me give you a tour."

The house consisted of the living room, dining room, kitchen, den, a master bedroom suite, a guest bedroom and another bathroom. A large patio extended across the back of the house and bordered along the edge of the swimming pool. They returned to the den, where Chance opened a bottle of wine and poured each of them a glass.

"I thought it would be nice to spend an evening at home—" An evening at home without the need of being entertained or relating to anything outside of each other. It felt so natural that the words just seemed to escape of their own accord. "I mean, we could maybe rent a video, or just listen to music. You know—" The embarrassment tried to take hold and he fought just as hard to shove it away. "Just spend some time together." He gestured toward the patio doors. "Would you like to go for a swim?"

She shook her head as she chuckled. "Going for a swim reminds me of something Glen said a couple of weeks ago. He's from Michigan and hasn't really adjusted to San Diego's winter weather. It's just a few days until the first of December and we're talking about swimming in the backyard pool."

"Well, it would be a shame to waste all this beautiful weather."

She looked at him in surprise. "You're serious?" Her manner was slightly flustered as she responded to his suggestion. "But I don't have a swimsuit with me."

"I have several guest swimsuits in the cabana out by the pool." He set his glass on the end table and pulled her into his arms. He whispered seductively into her ear. "Or we can leave the pool lights off and go skinny-dipping." He nuzzled her neck, then captured her mouth with an all-consuming kiss. He brushed his tongue against hers, the sensation exciting just as much as it did the first time.

There was nothing tentative or cautious about the passion that quickly exploded between them. She was in way over her head, but it was too late for it to matter. She knew she was falling in love with this dynamic man, but she did not have any idea what to do about it—or for that matter, whether she even wanted to do anything about it. She willingly gave herself over to the excitement he stirred in her.

He finally broke off the kiss, then tenderly cradled her head against his shoulder as he took a calming breath. "Marcie…" He took another deep breath, held it for several seconds, then slowly expelled it. "It's an unusually warm evening. Why don't we take our wine out to the patio? We can raid the refrigerator and try potluck for dinner."

It was as far removed from what he had wanted to say and do as was possible. He had been only a breath away from scooping her up in his arms and carrying her down the hall to his bedroom. But he didn't do it. He did not want her to think he had whisked her off to some *love lair* with nothing more on his mind than getting her into his bed as quickly as possible. She had already made it clear that she was well aware of the playboy reputation the tabloids had given him. He didn't want to give her cause to believe the description was accurate.

He had never been confused about how to proceed with a woman...until now. He wanted her more than he had ever wanted anyone. He wanted to intimately know all of her—her mind, her body and her soul—but the last thing he wanted was to make a wrong move with her and ruin whatever the future held. It was a problem that had never presented itself to him before. He always knew that if the current situation did not work out there was always another woman just around the bend.

He reluctantly reined in his libido and forced his thoughts toward more mundane matters— *safer* things that would not test his willpower or further inflame his desires for this very enticing woman. He released her from his embrace and picked up his wineglass. "Come on, let's go out to the patio."

Marcie was confused. A game? Was that what Chance was doing with her? Just playing a game? It didn't seem possible, not now that she had come to know the real man behind the tabloid headlines—or at least she thought she had. She had gotten the idea into her head that he had brought her to his house to make love to her, an enticing possibility that had danced through her mind with increased regularity over the past few days.

Her confusion carried over into her voice and across her face. "Chance? I don't understand—"

His last remnant of willpower vanished the second he looked into the depths of her eyes. He managed to set his glass of wine on the end table, although his movements were shaky at best. Then he pulled her into a crushing embrace. A strangled sound escaped his throat, something between a sigh and a groan.

He whispered the words, the sound tickling across her ear. "I didn't bring you here for the purpose of seducing you. Well, not exactly...not really. I'm not looking for childish games, or some coy little amusement merely to pass the time. Please believe that. I do want to make love to you, though, very much so." He placed a gentle kiss on her forehead. "But it has to be something you want, too."

Marcie squeezed her eyes shut and tried to get her thoughts together. He sounded so straightforward and so honest. She wanted to believe him. With all her heart she wanted to believe that this was not just a line he indiscriminately handed out to gullible women. She wanted very much for him to make love to her, but she did not want to be made a fool of. She tried to convince herself that was the reason for her concern.

She knew the truth, though. She knew she was just plain scared. She had never even dated anyone like Chance Fowler, let alone made love with someone so worldly and experienced. Her own insecurities left her feeling woefully inadequate. Then Hank Varney's words made their way back into her consciousness...Chance Fowler trusted her. Could she do any less in return?

She slipped her arms around his neck and reached her mouth up to his. A moment later his tongue brushed against hers, then all their heated passions burst into flame.

Chance pulled his head back from her, then cupped her face in his hands. His words came out in a husky whisper. ''You are a truly beautiful woman...a natural beauty, something real that's not wrapped in layers of phoniness and pretense. That's a truly rare quality in today's world.'' A wistful sigh crept into his voice. ''At least in the world where I seem to find myself more often than not.''

He gently ran his thumb across the kiss

swollen lushness of her lower lip. "I thought you were someone very special the instant I spotted you standing in front of that store window."

He clasped her hand in his and they walked down the hallway to the master bedroom suite, each with eyes wide open to the significance of the step they were about to take. The frantic rush of hormone-driven youth did not control their actions. It was a time for each and every step to be savored to the fullest.

Marcie paused at his bedroom door as a nervous anxiety began to tickle inside her.

He turned toward her with a questioning look. "Are you having second thoughts?"

Then his warm smile reached out and embraced her with a soothing comfort that told her she had nothing to fear. As quickly as the anxiety had appeared was the same speed with which it melted away, leaving her flushed with anticipation.

"No. No second thoughts."

A strange sensation nibbled at Chance's consciousness—nothing big and bothersome, but enough to get his attention. Nerves? If that was the case, then it would be the first time in many, many years that the prospect of making love to a desirable woman had made him nervous.

He grabbed the top edge of the bedspread from one side of the bed and Marcie took hold of it from the other side. They pulled it down to the foot of the king-size bed. He turned down the blanket and top sheet while Marcie fluffed the pillows. The sensation grew more insistent as the reality began to jell.

Yep, it was definitely nerves—no doubt about it. The far-reaching implications did not escape him, either. Making love to Marcie Roper mattered to him very much, which meant that she was far more important to his life than he had been willing to admit...even to himself. The knowledge did not sit comfortably with him.

Commitment and a committed relationship did not work. He had seen it for his entire life, most notably with his father's five—he corrected himself, *six* marriages. But it was also the case with most of his friends. There were far more divorces than happy marriages and a majority of those who were still married routinely cheated on their spouses—both husbands and wives. There was no reason to think it could work out any better for him.

He kicked off his shoes and pulled his shirt-tail from his jeans. He looked across the width of the bed and captured her gaze with his. It was an intimate moment of closeness even though no physical contact existed between them. He knelt on the bed and reached across to her, taking her hand into his. He brought it to his lips, then pulled her onto the bed and into his arms.

He held her tenderly in his embrace for what seemed like a very long time, even though in reality only a minute or two passed. He simply cradled her head against his shoulder and stroked her hair. Neither of them said a word. At that second he was more at one with her than he had ever been with another woman and that feeling washed away his doubts and concerns…at least for the moment.

Marcie snuggled into his arms. She had never felt as warm and protected in her entire adult life as she did locked away in his embrace. His lips brushed against her forehead. She wiggled her feet out of her shoes and shoved them off the bed with her bare foot.

His mouth came down on hers with an intense passion that swept through her body like wildfire. It stirred the energy surrounding them. They totally and fully succumbed to the desires and needs that had been subtly and not so subtly pushing and shoving at them. They sank into the softness of the bed.

Chance caressed her shoulders, her back, then finally ran his hand beneath her blouse and skimmed his fingers across her bare skin. Their tongues twined in a rhythmic dance ritual. Without breaking the passion of the kiss, he unbuttoned her blouse and slipped it off her shoulders.

Marcie did likewise, following Chance's lead by unbuttoning his shirt. Her fingertips tingled each time they came in contact with his well-defined chest. Her blood coursed hotly through her veins as she smoothed her hands across each tautly hewn plane and angle.

In spite of the nervousness each had experienced, the feeling of awkwardness that usually presented itself when two people made love for the first time did not materialize for them. Clothing fell away a piece at a time until bare skin touched bare skin along the length of their bodies. They very quickly became comfortable with each other—the sensual touch, the soft caress, the eager response—as if they were truly meant to be together.

His hand closed over her breast, the feel of her tightly puckered nipple teasing his already stimulated senses. He kissed behind her ear, the side of her neck, the base of her throat, then finally drew her nipple into his mouth. He held it there for a moment before releasing the tantalizing treat.

His voice surrounded her senses. ''Tell me where you want to be touched and how you want to be caressed. I want to know every secret place that excites you.''

Her words were undeniably sincere while containing a breathless excitement. ''I've never had anyone say that to me before.''

''Then the others were fools for not wanting to please you in every way possible.'' They were the last coherent words he was able to get out of his mouth.

She ran her hands through his hair, caressed his strong shoulders and back. Her nipples tingled with each demand of his mouth. Every place he touched her acted as a conduit allowing sexual energy to leap between them. Each fed off the other's increasing levels of passion and desire.

She shuddered as his hand moved slowly up her inner thigh, his fingers lightly tickling the sensitive skin. He drew his fingers through the dark downy softness, then slipped between the warm moist folds of her womanhood. Her mouth went dry as scorching sensations touched every fiber of her existence.

Chance nuzzled her neck, kissed her throat and then moved his lips sensually over her body, savoring the silkiness of her skin until he arrived at the hot core of her sexual being. Her low throaty moan of pleasure reached his ears as he bestowed the most intimate kiss of all.

She totally abandoned herself to the delicious sensations. Her mind, her body—her entire being fused into one under his expert touch. Her words were a breathless whisper. "Oh, Chance...I've never felt like this before." She rubbed her hand across his chest, tracing patterns on his skin, her hand moving in an ever-widening circle. Her fingers skimmed across his hard flat belly, moving closer to the manhood rising between his thighs.

He wanted to consume her in an explosion of unrestrained passion. As her fingers moved across his belly, he felt tremors start deep inside him, radiating down through his thighs and up through his chest. He recaptured her delicately pointed nipple with his mouth and cupped her other breast in the warmth of his hand, marveling at how perfectly it fit. He trembled as her fingers brushed across his groin, then returned to gently stroke his hardened arousal. His nerve endings were on fire. Her touch did magical things to his senses.

He stroked the length of her body, his hand finally cupping the roundness of her bottom. He wanted to touch all of her at once, to stimulate every hidden place that excited her, to revel in the intimacy of that excitement.

She had never before experienced anything like Chance Fowler. He was the most giving, unselfish lover she had ever known. His sole concern seemed to be what pleased her and what type of pleasure he could give her next.

She continued to gently stroke his arousal, sending quivering sensations through his body. She laid a trail of hot kisses across his chest and down his belly as her lips moved over his taut body. She dipped her head lower and provocatively tasted his hardness as she lightly brushed her fingertips across his chest.

His head jerked back in the pillow, his eyes squeezed tightly shut. An intense growl of pleasure rose from his throat. He lifted her to him and laid her back on the bed with her head resting lightly on the pillow. He reached his hand to the nightstand, pulled open the top drawer and withdrew a packet.

A minute later he placed his knee between her thighs, opening her to his probing desire. As his lips nibbled at her mouth, his hardness slowly penetrated the velvety soft heat of her body. The first rush of pleasurable sensations was so intense that it took his breath away. He set what started out as a slow, sensual rhythm but quickly escalated as the rapture built. She met every thrust of his hips with an equal one of her own.

As she welcomed his burning hardness into her most intimate recess, she experienced a surge of sensual delight unlike anything she had ever before known. Her gasp of pleasure was cut off as his mouth came down on hers hot and insistent.

Marcie soared beyond what she thought was possible. He propelled her over the crest of everything she had ever imagined. The electrifying sensations rapidly built, one on top of the other. The incendiary feelings were so intense she was unable to keep them in. She cried out as the ultimate rapture carried her beyond the limits. She held on to him as if he were life itself.

Chance held her tightly as his own rapture teetered on the brink. He threw his head back as release shuddered through him. He called out her name, then buried his face in the feathery tresses of her hair as the surges subsided.

They remained connected in the warm afterglow of their union, neither wanting to let go of the other. She lay beneath him, her body satiated by his lovemaking, her arms wound tightly around his neck, her legs tangled with his. He lay on top of her, afraid to move, afraid to break the tangible connection that joined their bodies and the intangible thread that bound their souls.

The only sounds in the room were Marcie's and Chance's attempts to return their breathing to normal. They remained in his bed, his arms wrapped protectively around her body as she snuggled against his warmth. He stroked her hair and trailed his fingers across the creamy smoothness of her skin. There was no awkwardness attached to the silence that surrounded them—at least not outwardly.

Chance was physically relaxed, but his

thoughts were bouncing around inside his head at full speed. There was no doubt in his mind that Marcie was the only woman for him. She offered everything missing in his life. She was a hard worker, an independent woman with a strong sense of self. She had an identity of her own and did not need to hang on to him or cling to his every move and word. How different she was from most women he'd met. And she certainly was nothing like his so-called stepmothers. Three of his father's six wives had been clinging vines without an original thought in their heads. Marcie, on the other hand, knew how to take care of herself— a fair and honest person without pretenses.

His personal observations of family life, especially his father's example, had left him believing that the concept of maintaining a successful relationship was a myth rather than part of normal life.

So he continued to hold her tightly in his arms and said nothing.

Marcie's mind floated on a cloud of euphoria. She did not think she had ever been happier or more content than she was at that precise moment. She suspected—no, she more than suspected. She *knew* she was falling in love with Chance Fowler. It was not the Chance Fowler whose exploits were in the newspapers, nor the one who was heir to a family fortune, and certainly not the one who had been so sure of himself that he had brazenly grabbed her on a city street and kissed her.

Her Chance Fowler was the man who had driven to Crestview Bay just to return her books when he could have mailed them, the one who provided training and employment for those in need while going out of his way to shun all publicity and recognition for his good deeds, the one who asked to make love to her rather than assume she would automatically allow it.

It was finally Chance who broke the silence. He kissed her tenderly on the forehead, then ran his hand down her back and across the curve of her bottom. His voice was thick with the passion that continued to stir inside him. "Stay the night with me. I want to make love to you again and again."

Her immediate response was a soft moan of pleasure when he teased her nipple with his tongue. She rubbed her foot against his calf. "The entire night?"

"Tomorrow is a holiday. You don't have to go to work, and you've already said you don't have any plans. We're going sailing tomorrow, so you might as well spend the night here."

"But I don't have any clean clothes to put on, or any—"

"There goes that serious, logical nature of yours." He brushed a soft kiss against her lips to hush her objections. "All right, but this is my one and only offer of a compromise. We can go back to your place in the morning and you can change clothes and do whatever it is you need to do." He flashed an impish grin. "*Then* we'll go sailing."

She returned a teasing smile. "You sound as if you've made all the decisions. There doesn't seem to be anything left for me to do other than agree." She playfully nibbled on his earlobe.

He tucked a loose tendril of hair behind her ear, then brushed his fingertips across her cheek. His voice became soft, his manner caring. "Is there something you'd like? Anything I can get for you?" His manner brightened. He quickly sat upright. "I know...I'll bet you're hungry. I did promise you something to eat and I know I'm hungry." He turned loose of her and swung his legs over the side of the bed, then rose to his feet. ''I'll see what I can find in the kitchen.''

He leaned over the bed and placed a loving kiss on her mouth. He started to pull back, but allowed his lips to linger against hers a moment longer. ''I'll be right back.''

Marcie nestled into the softness of the bed as she watched Chance leave the bedroom. The sensual afterglow of their lovemaking still clung to her senses and warmed her heart. She may have been confused and uncertain about her feelings before they made love, but things jumped into crystal clarity the moment they had become one. All of her lingering doubts about whether or not she was falling for him were swept aside. There was no longer any question attached to her feelings. Plain and simple—she loved Chance Fowler.

She pulled the blanket up to her neck and closed her eyes. She encouraged the smile that tugged at the corners of her mouth. She felt protected, safe, cared for—enclosed in a cocoon woven from the fabric of love. She did not know what the future held, but as long as that future included Chance Fowler, everything would be perfect. An errant thought tickled at the back of her mind, a gray cloud that tried to push its way into her reality. She refused to acknowledge its existence, choosing instead to shove it away as she snuggled deeper into the security of Chance's bed.

Chance's thoughts were not as euphoric as Marcie's. As soon as he reached the kitchen he poured himself a glass of wine. He stood at the patio door and stared out at the swimming pool. Making love with her had produced an unsettlingly profound effect. He could not deny that she meant more to him than anyone else ever had, but just how much that was had him rattled.

He was thirty-six years old and had never been truly in love in his entire life. He had certainly been in lust more times than he could remember, and even temporarily enamored on several occasions—but never in love. Was this what love felt like? The thrill and excitement of just being with her, touching her, hearing her voice, was almost overwhelming. On the other hand, the magnitude of what it all meant was equally overwhelming. It meant a commitment to the type of relationship that could only lead to marriage. Was he capable of overcoming his negative thoughts and feelings where marriage was concerned to make a commitment that would last a lifetime?

The thoughts swirled around inside his head as he continued to stare out the sliding-glass door. He knew what he wanted, but he did not know if he could do what he needed to do to achieve it. Would Marcie possibly be willing to just live with him to test whether a relationship could be sustained? Would it be fair to her to even ask such a thing?

''Chance?''

Her voice startled him out of his thoughts. He whirled around and immediately spotted her standing across the room. She looked deliciously sexy and incredibly desirable. Her mussed hair only added to the allure of someone who looked as if she had just gotten out of bed and should be back there with someone to keep her company. As she crossed the room he spotted the note of caution in her eyes.

"Is everything all right? You didn't come back to the bedroom. I was concerned."

He pulled her to him. His words choked off in his throat, the only sound a soft moan as he captured her face in his trembling hands. His gaze pierced right through her, descending into the very depths of her soul. He backed her up against the pantry door as his mouth came down on hers.

She felt the heat radiating from his touch. A weakness developed in her legs and quickly spread throughout her body. Only the support of the pantry door and Chance's weight leaning against her kept Marcie from collapsing under the spell he cast over her. She reached her arms around his neck as she opened her mouth to the probing of his searing tongue— every nerve ending tingled, every fiber of her body aflame. She was barely cognizant of his hands leaving her face until his fingers made scalding ripples every place they touched her skin—her breasts, her back, her hips, her bottom, the flat of her stomach and her inner thighs.

Chance had never been so totally consumed by uncontrolled passion. He placed his hands at her waist and lifted her off the floor. She responded by wrapping her legs around his hips. A moment later he filled her with a smooth upward thrust of his hardness. He felt the fire of her soul race from the depths of her core through the private recess of their intimate joining directly to his heart.

Seven

Chance took a quick look at the kitchen clock before stepping outside to the darkened patio. It was almost five in the morning. It would be a while yet before the dawn light brightened the night sky. He had been careful not to wake Marcie when he slipped out of bed. There was no reason for her to be awake simply because he could not sleep.

Their night together had been everything he had hoped it would be…and everything he feared it might be. He was enthralled, elated, ecstatic…and in love.

And he was scared to death.

He could not imagine life without Marcie Roper, but he did not know if he could do what needed to be done to ensure that it would always be that way. He did not know if he was capable of making a lifelong commitment to her and to a relationship—a lifelong commitment that should mean marriage. How could he rationalize the way he felt when he believed that marriage was nothing more than a worthless piece of paper?

He stood at the edge of the pool staring at the water. Life would have been so much simpler if only he had allowed the photographer to take his picture. He executed a dive from the edge of the pool and swam the length under water. He had hoped it would wash away his doubts and concerns, but he had been mistaken. When he surfaced at the other end, nothing had changed. He ducked back under water and shoved off again.

When he resurfaced this time he saw Marcie standing on the pool deck, looking down at him. She had taken his shirt and wrapped it around her like a robe. She looked as if she'd just woken up, her face still carrying the residual signs of sleep. He felt the swell of emotion surge through his body the moment he focused in on her.

''I'm sorry if I woke you up. I tried to be

as quiet as I could.'' He moved through the water along the edge of the pool until he reached the place where she stood.

''You didn't wake me.'' She extended a warm smile. ''How long have you been up?'' Her heart fluttered with excitement as she sat on the edge of the pool and dangled her legs in the surprisingly warm water.

''Not very long.'' He playfully tugged on her ankle as he shot her a decidedly lascivious look. ''Why don't you join me? It won't be daylight for a little while yet, so you won't need to find a swimsuit.'' He ran his hand along the curve of her calf, then nestled his body at the edge of the pool between her legs. Her excitement increased as he slid his hands along her thighs, then up under the shirt.

She could barely catch her breath as he planted his forearms on the decking on either side of her and raised his body up out of the water. He leaned forward and nuzzled his face into the opening of the shirt. A tingle of anticipation settled low inside her as his mouth found her nipple.

She was not sure whether he pulled her into the water or whether she slipped off the edge of the pool, but whichever way it was, she ended up with her body sandwiched between his body and the wall of the pool. His mouth was on hers and a moment later all the passion from the night before ignited inside her.

It was almost sunset when Marcie and Chance left the yacht club after making sure the *Celeste* was securely docked. They walked to his car hand in hand. He paused before opening the car door for her and folded her into his embrace.

"Thank you for spending the day with me."

"Thank you for taking me sailing. I've never been out on a sailboat before. I can see why you enjoy it so much. And I really enjoyed meeting Dave and Bonnie. They seem like very nice people."

"They are nice people, and I know they enjoyed meeting you, too." He brushed a soft kiss against her lips. His voice dropped to a mere whisper. "Thank you for spending last night with me."

Nothing more was said as he drove her to her house. They were each lost in very personal thoughts of the future and what it held. They finally arrived at Marcie's house. He walked her to the door, continuing to grasp her hand in his so that she could not go inside when he paused on the porch.

He caressed her cheek, then cupped her chin in his hand. "Do you think I could talk you into spending tonight with me, too?"

As much as his suggestion appealed to her, she knew she had to get her head back into reality. "Even though we were closed today for the Thanksgiving holiday, we will be open tomorrow. In the same way that shopping malls consider the Friday after Thanksgiving to be the biggest single shopping day of the year, it's also a busy day for us, since most people have a four day weekend."

"Okay." He pulled her into his arms. "How about I spend the night with you?" He brushed a soft kiss on her lips.

Marcie rested her head against his shoulder. Her mind was in a whirl and she didn't know how to respond to him. As much as the thought of spending another night with Chance Fowler inflamed her already considerable desires, everything had happened so quickly that she knew she needed to step back and catch her breath.

When she did not give him an immediate answer Chance took that as a bad sign. He took the key from her hand, unlocked her front door, and the two of them went inside. He put his arms around her, held her closely, and whispered in her ear. "About my suggestion...you haven't given me an answer." He kissed her behind the ear. "I would like very much to spend the night here with you."

"I'm not..." She paused as she tried to collect her thoughts and turn them into intelligent words. "I have a very busy day on tap for tomorrow. I think I'd better get a good night's sleep." She saw the disappointment spread across his face. Had he misunderstood her intentions? A sense of urgency crept into her voice as she slipped her arms around his waist. "You do understand, don't you?"

"Sure. I have several things to do, too." His voice conveyed the same disappointment that showed on his face. Then he added cautiously, "How about dinner tomorrow night? Or maybe a movie?"

"Yes." She extended a smile filled with warmth and a hint of a soft sensuality. "I'd like that...very much."

Chance lingered for a few more minutes, then kissed her good-night and left. Marcie watched as he pulled out of her driveway and drove down the street. She closed and locked the door.

It had been the most incredible night of her life. By the time dawn colored the morning sky they had made love three times...each experience more intense and meaningful for her than the previous one. But she felt as if she had been on some kind of whirlwind adventure that was not part of her normal life. She knew she needed to step back and center herself in reality again. She was a sensible, logical woman. Having roots and a stable home life was very important to her, and as far as she could tell, Chance Fowler offered neither of those things.

Unfortunately, there was nothing sensible or logical about him or the way he made her feel every time he so much as looked at her, let alone touched her. Could her reality continue to include him? She did not know what the future held, but she certainly hoped Chance would be a part of it. She also knew there was a large chasm between what she wanted out of life and the type of life-style that belonged to him. It was a problem that she knew would give her many sleepless nights. It was also a problem that she knew they would one day need to confront. What would happen then?

Her euphoria over being in love had become tempered by the reality of what she feared. She walked to her bedroom as she unbuttoned her blouse. She decided to slip into her robe and read for a while.

Marcie was not the only one with her mind on the future. Chance was every bit as bothered and concerned as she was. He drove toward San Diego and home, but his mind was cluttered with his confusion about what to do. He knew what was happening to him. He was falling in love with Marcie Roper—more precisely, he had already fallen in love with her—straightforward, plain and simple. But he didn't know what to do about it, or even if he wanted it to be so.

As soon as Chance arrived home he was thrown back into the real world by two phone messages on his answering machine. One was from Scott Blake in San Francisco and the other was from Anne Metcalfe, his father's longtime secretary. He took care of them in order of importance to him. He returned Scott's call first.

''Scott, it's Chance. What can I do for you?

Is there a problem with the Oakland property?''

''No problem. We're moving along faster than I thought we would. I need you to do another walk-through and sign off on what we've done. When can you come up here?''

''Let me check my schedule and get back to you first thing in the morning, if that's okay.'' He quickly concluded his conversation. He hadn't planned on making a trip to the Bay area so soon.

He started to return Anne Metcalfe's call but decided against it. It was Thanksgiving Day when even his father's most loyal employees should have been off work, but Anne was dutifully following his instructions. Her message did not mention anything about a problem, so whatever his father wanted could wait until the morning. His thoughts were still with Marcie and what to do about something that would have had most people jumping with joy—what to do about being in love.

Maybe things would be clearer in the morning after a good night's sleep. He took care of a few other business matters, got something to eat, then went to his bedroom. He sat on the edge of the bed and ran his hands across the rumpled sheets. It was where he and Marcie had made love for the first and second times. The third time had been just before sunrise out by the pool. Never before had anyone filled his heart with so much joy and so completely fulfilled his every desire.

He sat lost in thought as the uncertainty churned inside him. He emitted a sigh of resignation as he reached for the phone. He was pretty sure he knew why Anne Metcalfe had called him. He might as well return her call and get it over with. He dialed the number and waited for someone to answer.

"Anne. It's Chance." His voice held all the weariness that he had forced into the background while he was enjoying a fun day of sailing with Marcie. But now that he was alone it had managed to seep back into his consciousness.

"You have orders from on high for the annual festivities?" He could not resist the touch of sarcasm. "I assume I'm being instructed to report to the family enclave for another touching holiday get-together and to sit for the photographer for a new family portrait. After all, last year's portrait contained Mrs. Douglas Fowler number five. We wouldn't want Joan to feel left out, since she's the one who currently holds that exalted position.''

''Now, Chance. It's Christmas. This is the one time of year that's important to your father to have family gathered together—''

''Oh, Anne...'' He tried to suppress his cynicism as he shook his head in dismay. ''I don't know how much dear ol' Dad pays you, but it's not nearly enough. He has plenty of family without needing to concern himself with me. All my aunts and uncles will be there, along with all my cousins and my cousin's children. Each and every one of them will be vying for his time and a stake in the family fortune. I'm not interested in being around all that phoniness and I certainly don't need or want any of his money.''

''Uh, speaking of money. Your father wanted me to ask why you returned the birthday check he mailed you last month.''

''Like I said...I don't need or want his money. I do okay on my own without him.''

''But it was a birthday present—''

There was a sharp edge of disgust to his voice. ''It was a cold, impersonal check signed by his corporate controller and mailed out from his accounting department—no different than the checks he sends out to pay his bills. I'm not a bill that needs to be paid." He took a calming breath. "I don't mean to be rude, Anne, but I'm tired. Could you just give me my holiday instructions without trying to explain my father to me?"

"Your father has decided on December 6th for this year's get-together. That's a week from this Sunday. He will be expecting you at one o'clock for the social gathering and dinner will be served at four o'clock. The children's presents will be opened at six o'clock and the adults will exchange their gifts at nine o'clock."

"That's almost three weeks before Christmas. Why so early?"

"Your father and Joan won't be here for the holidays. They're planning to spend Christmas and New Year's in Tahiti. Does that date work with your schedule?"

"I'll make sure that it does." He made no attempt to hide the sarcasm that surrounded his words. "I wouldn't want to miss dear ol' Dad's annual Christmas extravaganza."

After hanging up the phone Chance transferred the information to his calendar. He had been aware of the strain in Anne's voice as she gave him the date and time for Christmas dinner. The guilt washed over him. There was no reason for him to have been so caustic with her. She was just doing her job. He would make it up to her. Maybe one of those cute I'm-sorry-for-acting-like-a-jerk greeting cards along with some flowers.

As Marcie had predicted, the Friday after Thanksgiving was a busy day for the nursery. There were customers waiting at the door when she opened for business at eight o'clock that morning and things continued brisk until after lunch. She took advantage of a midafternoon lull in the stream of customers to remove the Thanksgiving seasonal merchandise and replace it with the remainder of the Christmas items. She also worked on the invitation for the annual employee and customer Christmas party at her house. She had been so busy that she was surprised when Glen wandered toward the front desk dressed to leave.

"Well, everything in back is secured and everyone else has already gone home. Is there anything you need before I go?"

She extended a weary smile. "Nothing at all. Good night, Glen. I'll see you tomorrow."

She locked the front door behind him and began her daily close-out procedures at the cash register. She had not heard from Chance all day. She thought they had a date for that night; at least they had talked about it when he had taken her home last night even though they hadn't decided on anything specific. She kept glancing out the front window, expecting to see him drive up any minute, but he never appeared. There was nothing left to do but set the alarm and leave.

She drove directly home, berating herself the entire way about her feelings of disappointment because she had not heard from Chance. She knew she needed to get herself under control. She could not center her life and feelings around whether or not Chance Fowler attempted to make contact with her each and every day. After all, it had been less than twenty-four hours since she had last seen him.

She tried to dismiss it from her mind. She had plenty to do to keep her busy. She'd set her company Christmas party for Monday, December 14th, at six o'clock at her house. She needed to have the client invitations in the mail tomorrow morning. She'd brought her list home and needed only to address the envelopes and put on the stamps. She'd already apprised her employees of the date and time and would include an invitation in their next paychecks.

She looked around her house. That left only the job of holiday decorations. She knew she couldn't put it off any longer. She set about the task of addressing the invitations. As soon as she finished, she took the Christmas decorations out of her storage closet and began unpacking them. The ringing phone interrupted the chore.

''Hello?''

Chance's smooth voice came across the phone line. ''Hi. I hope I'm not interrupting anything important.''

She could not stop the smile that turned up the corners of her mouth and the warm feeling that flooded through her body. ''Nothing that can't wait.''

''I wanted to get by before you closed, but I was in a meeting that ran long. Do you still want to go out tonight?''

She glanced around the room at the clutter. ''I think I'm too far into the mess I've made to stop now. Would you mind if we did it some other time?''

"You sound a little tired. How was your day?"

"It was busy. In fact—" she glanced at the stack of envelopes ready to go in the mail "—I even brought some work home with me."

"Really?" A gentle teasing quality surrounded his words. "I thought the boss was supposed to delegate the workload rather than have to take it home."

A soft chuckle escaped her throat. "Maybe that's the way it works in big business, but not for the small business owner."

"I have to go to San Francisco on business in the next day or so. Since you won't go out with me tonight, do you suppose I could talk you into going to San Francisco with me?"

"Well...I don't know. I do have a business to run and—"

"We can leave as soon as you close on Saturday and spend Saturday night in San Francisco. I can take care of my business on Sunday and we can fly home on Sunday night. How does that sound?"

She closed her eyes for a moment as she tried to control the excitement that welled inside her. She didn't need to be at the nursery on Sunday. "Yes, that sounds like fun."

They talked for a few minutes longer before hanging up. She was a sensible woman who did not fly off on last-minute weekend jaunts to San Francisco, yet that was exactly what she had agreed to do. And the most remarkable thing about it was the fact that she did not feel guilty about indulging the frivolous pleasure. Marcie returned her attention to the Christmas decorations, her spirit much lighter than it had been before Chance's call.

She draped evergreen garland around the fireplace, replaced several things on the mantel with Christmas items, hung a large wreath on the front door, and arranged holiday candles on the coffee table. She tied large red bows along the front porch railing and on the corner beams of the back patio. All that was left was to put a tree in the living room in front of the large window and decorate it. There was plenty of time for that yet. She glanced at the clock and was surprised to find that it was going on midnight.

She quickly got ready for bed and snuggled under the covers. She turned her thoughts to Chance Fowler and their weekend in San Francisco. She wondered what kind of business he could be conducting on a Sunday. Her eyelids grew heavy as the soft warmth settled over her. Going away for the weekend together, making passionate love with Chance—it was more than she ever dreamed possible.

Sleep finally claimed her. Sensual and erotic dreams revolving around Chance Fowler played over and over in her mind.

Chance carried the overnight bags as they exited the plane through the jetway. They hurried through the airport, picked up the rental car, and were soon traveling north from the San Francisco airport into town. It was not until he turned toward the Golden Gate Bridge continuing north out of San Francisco that Marcie questioned where they were going.

"I thought you said you had a condo in San Francisco?"

"The San Francisco Bay area in general, but specifically it's just across the bridge in Tiburon. We'll be there in a few minutes."

Chance pulled the car into the garage of the town house. A few minutes later they stood on the balcony.

"Oh, Chance...this is an incredible view of San Francisco. All the city lights spread out across the horizon. It's stunning." Marcie took in a deep breath, filling her lungs with the ocean air. "I could look at this forever."

He stood behind her, his arms around her waist and his head resting against hers. "I bought this condo when it was still under construction. I took one look at the view and knew I had to have it." He nuzzled her neck then kissed her cheek. He felt her shiver as the chilly night air settled over them.

His words tickled across her ear. "It's a lot colder here than San Diego. Let's go inside. We can snuggle in front of a cozy fire in the fireplace." He turned her around in his arms until she faced him. He brushed a loving kiss across her lips. His voice dropped to a soft whisper. "Better yet, we can make love in front of the fireplace. How does that plan sound to you?"

She closed her eyes and rested her head against his shoulder while slipping her arms around his waist. A warm feeling of contentment flowed through her body. "It sounds wonderful."

As before, it was a night that met and fulfilled each and every expectation. It was a time of sensuality and intimacy, a time not to be rushed but rather to be savored to the fullest.

Soft kisses and gentle caresses slowly gave way to a greater sense of urgency as their passion escalated. As before, their lovemaking transported each of them to a level of emotional sharing that neither had ever before achieved. It also solidified their love for each other, washing away any remaining doubts about whether it was a temporary infatuation or the real thing. However, it was a love that still remained unspoken.

They slept that night wrapped in each other's arms and woke to a bright sunny day. They carried their coffee out to the balcony in order to enjoy the crisp morning air and beautiful daytime view of the San Francisco skyline across the bay.

Chance watched as she sipped her coffee. He took her hand in his, kissed her palm, then laced their fingers together. A thought had been forming in the back of his mind. Bolstered by the lingering afterglow of their lovemaking that still clung to his senses, he decided to act on it.

He nervously cleared his throat. "Do you have any plans for next Sunday, as in one week from today?"

"Nothing I'm aware of right now. Why?"

He extended a warm smile. "Good. Dear ol' Dad is having the annual family Christmas dinner get-together next Sunday and I would be very pleased if you would be my guest."

She was unable to hide her surprise. "You mean, you want to take me to meet your family?"

"Well, sort of…" It was not the response he had anticipated. It had not occurred to him that she would interpret his desire to have one friendly face at the dinner table as him taking her home to meet the family. He saw the confusion come into her eyes.

"'Sort of'? I don't understand."

He forced a laugh, hoping it would sound casual. "I didn't mean that *sort of* the way it sounded. I only meant that I wanted the pleasure of your company—one smiling, beautiful face to lift the day out of the doldrums and bring it into the sunshine."

She cocked her head and stared at him for a moment. His words may have been light, but the caution buried in the depths of his eyes told another story. It was as if she had tapped into the persona behind the facade, as if she could feel his inner sorrow. She certainly understood about the loneliness of the holiday season. "That's kind of a sad statement."

Rather than immediately respond to her comment, he leaned his face into hers and placed a tender kiss on her mouth. He allowed his lips to linger against hers for a moment, then recaptured her mouth with more intensity. He pulled her into his arms, ran his fingers through her hair, then cradled her head against his shoulder. His voice was quiet, leaving no doubt about his sincerity. "I didn't mean for it to sound that way. I only meant that you would be a welcome breath of fresh air to the traditional dinner table and I'd very much enjoy having you accompany me."

"Well, how could anyone object to being called a breath of fresh air?" She extended a radiant smile. "I'd be very honored to join you."

Several minutes of quiet togetherness held them as if they were in a secluded cove far removed from the turmoil of the surroundings. She pondered the significance of his inviting her to his father's house for a family holiday function. Was it no more than what he had said, or did she dare to hope it was more? Things between them had happened so suddenly and had exploded into a very deep and meaningful relationship so quickly. At least that was the way it had happened for her—quick, powerful, and totally unexpected, like wildfire. Would it end up in ashes when it had finally run its course?

Chance finally broke the moment of quiet intimacy. ''I have to meet Scott Blake in one hour. We're going to take a look at a house in Oakland that I'm having remodeled. I need to sign off on the work that's already been done. Would you like to go along or would you rather stay here and relax? I'll only be gone a couple of hours.''

''I'd like to go with you, if that's okay.''

''Of course it's okay.'' He kissed her on the forehead, then went to take a shower.

Chance stood in the hot water, allowing it to wash over his head and down his body. He was not sure exactly why he had invited Marcie to his father's house. It certainly wasn't to share any close feelings of the family gathering. It was as if she was his link to what life could be, to what it would be like to be part of a real family. He shook away the feeling of foreboding that shivered through his consciousness. He hoped he had not made a mistake in judgment by letting his father know that there was someone special in his life.

He quickly dried himself and dressed. He didn't want to be away from Marcie any longer than absolutely necessary.

They had breakfast at a small restaurant overlooking the water, then met Scott Blake at the Oakland house. After introductions were made, Scott took them through the house.

"This looks great, Scott. The guys have really done a good job. It looks like you'll be finished in a couple of weeks. I'll check with my real estate broker about whether it should go on the market immediately or wait until after the holidays. Meanwhile, I'll get him looking for another place for me." Chance signed the appropriate paperwork, then he and Marcie told Scott goodbye.

He reached over and grasped her hand as he drove. "It's not even noon yet and our flight isn't until ten tonight. Is there anything special you'd like to do today or any place in particular you'd like to go?"

"Is there enough time to take a tour of one of the wineries in Napa or Sonoma?"

Chance glanced at his watch then gave her a smile. "Yes, there's time. And if there isn't, the worst thing that can happen is we catch the first flight out tomorrow morning rather than fly back tonight.''

He headed the car toward wine country. It had all the makings of a beautiful day spent with the woman he loved. What could be better? A little trickle of concern tried to seep into his happy thoughts; a concern about introducing Marcie to his father. But as he had before, he shoved the whisper of irritation aside, convincing himself that it was nothing more than the normal anxiety that accompanied each face-to-face encounter with his father.

As he had hoped, the day proved to be one filled with pure fun. They toured a winery, then Chance surprised her with a hot air balloon ride over Napa Valley, culminating at sunset. He reveled in the excitement and pleasure that radiated from her face. He had never felt so much at one with another human being. He had never known what true love was until now.

Eight

———

Lunchtime Monday found Marcie rushing home from the nursery. It had been so late when they arrived at the San Diego airport the night before that she had agreed to spend the night at Chance's house. Then he'd driven her to Crestview Bay that morning. The flush of excitement from their San Francisco adventure still clung to her senses as she tried to concentrate on the day's business.

The real Chance Fowler was so far removed from the headline-grabbing playboy that she had first encountered, it was as if they were not even part of the same world. Her Chance Fowler was considerate and caring yet had an unpredictable streak and a sense of uninhibited fun. And she loved him so very much. Was it possible to love someone too much? She knew she was too involved to turn back.

While she was home she grabbed a few of the Christmas party invitations and drove to the cottage Chance was having remodeled. She spotted Hank Varney's truck in the driveway. She parked and hurried inside.

"Hank? Do you have a minute?"

He turned around at the sound of his name. "Sure, Marcie. What can I do for you?"

"Every year I host a Christmas party for my employees and select clients. I'd like to invite you and your crew to join us this year." She handed him the invitations. "This will give you the time and place. I look forward to seeing you there."

Hank took the invitations from her. She saw the surprise on his face quickly turn to pleasure. "Thanks, Marcie. This is very nice of you. I look forward to it."

She exchanged a few more words with Hank, then went out to the backyard to talk to Eric Ross, the head of her landscaping crew.

"How's it going, Eric?" She looked around, determining the amount of progress they'd made on the project.

"It's coming along just fine. It's nice to be able to do something of this size without the owner hanging over our shoulders questioning every move we make."

"I just invited Hank and his crew to the company Christmas party. If anyone shows any concern about what to wear, make sure you let them know that it's very casual and relaxed."

"Sure thing." Eric started to return to his work, then paused and turned back toward Marcie. "Here's something you might mention to Glen. One of the construction guys, his name's Bob, seems real interested in the landscaping stuff we're doing. He asked lots of questions about the nursery and I get the impression that he might like to have a job there. He seems like a decent guy and he's a hard worker. Maybe Glen can take some time to talk to him at the party."

"I'll mention it to him as soon as I get back. This increased workload is beginning to get him down. I hope he finds someone to hire soon or he'll end up working himself into a sickbed."

The entire week moved along quickly. Marcie's days were busy at work, but her nights belonged to Chance. They'd often don warm jackets and take late-night walks along the moonlit beach. They went out to dinner one night. They rented a couple of movies and stayed home another night. It did not seem to matter what they did or where they went, as long as they were together. Marcie had never been happier in her entire life.

Chance, too, had become totally enmeshed in the web of love that surrounded them. However, as the week drew to a close he began to feel edgy. His misgiving over the dinner at his father's house and having involved Marcie in it began to show, especially the Saturday night before the Sunday event.

They had been to a movie and stopped to get something to eat before he drove her home. He walked her to the front door.

"You've been very quiet, Chance. Is there something wrong?"

He brought her hand to his lips and placed a kiss on her palm. It seemed to be more of an absentminded gesture than an intentional show of affection.

"Chance?" When he did not respond to her question she became a little more emphatic.

"Are you okay, Chance? Is something wrong?"

"Huh?" His attention snapped back to the present as he suddenly became aware of what she said. "I'm sorry, I guess my mind was elsewhere."

"Anything you'd care to talk about?" A little tickle of anxiety tried to push its way to the forefront.

"Not really... Well, I mean I was just concerned that maybe you were feeling obligated to accompany me to the dinner tomorrow. It's not that big a deal, and I can assure you it will not be an enjoyable afternoon and evening. If you'd rather not go, please say so. I'd certainly understand."

The hint of anxiety grew stronger. She tried to sound casual and upbeat while she searched for the hidden truth. "It sounds like you're trying to say you don't want me to go." She hesitated for a moment, not sure whether to say any more. She tentatively ventured her question. "Would you rather I didn't go?"

He placed a soft kiss on her mouth. He saw the disappointment in her eyes and heard it in her voice. He tried to project a confident smile and attitude. "Of course I want you to go with me. I was just concerned that you might be uncomfortable or bored. I just didn't want you to feel obligated, that's all.''

Her words were tentative. ''Are you sure?''

''Positive.'' He pulled her into his embrace and held her body tightly against his. He wished he was half as sure about bringing Marcie and his father together as he pretended to be. He was not even sure exactly why the concern continued to pick at him, but it did.

Chance pulled his car into the circular drive in front of the large house surrounded by meticulously manicured grounds. Several cars were parked along the edges of the driveway. It looked as if most of the family members had already assembled. The agitation churned in the pit of his stomach. There was nothing he wanted to do at that moment more than to turn around and drive away from that house, from the people assembled there, from his father's edict that they gather for the annual family Christmas dinner. He took a deep breath, clenched his jaw as he slowly exhaled, then turned toward Marcie. He forced a smile.

''Well...here we are.'' A nervous chuckle

escaped his throat. "Dear ol' Dad's idea of *home sweet home.*"

Marcie had been aware of the tension coursing through Chance from the moment he picked her up. An edge of sarcasm seemed to cling to him that almost bordered on the cynical. She had silently vowed to project only good humor and an upbeat attitude. She could truly empathize with his feelings about the holidays being a stressful time and she did not want to add to his obviously distressed condition.

"Marcie..." He turned toward her, making no move to get out of the car. He brushed his fingertips across her cheek, then tucked a stray lock of hair behind her ear as he searched her face and eyes. He found the understanding he sought and it kindled a warm spot deep inside him. "I know I've been in a lousy mood. This annual holiday command appearance ritual always sets me on edge." He allowed a soft chuckle to escape his throat. "I don't know whether to apologize for subjecting you to this or thank you for agreeing to be here. I guess what I need to do is both. I'm sure you're not going to find this much of a picnic, but your presence will certainly lighten my day." He leaned his face into hers and placed a loving kiss on her lips.

She returned his kiss. "It's my pleasure."

He gave an apologetic shrug and extended a sheepish grin. "I sincerely doubt that it will be." He took a calming breath, then spoke with as much enthusiasm as he could force into his voice. "Well, shall we go inside?" He got out of the car, held her door open for her, then escorted her up the steps toward the front entrance.

As they approached, the large double doors swung open, revealing an imposing figure of a man standing on the other side. There was no doubt in Marcie's mind that this was Douglas Winston Fowler. The physical resemblance between father and son was unmistakable. But where Chance's sky-blue eyes crinkled with amusement and showed a caring nature, his father's ice-blue eyes revealed an uncompromising hardness and his practiced smile carried no warmth.

Douglas Fowler stepped forward to greet his guests. "It's good to see you, Chance." He turned toward Marcie, his gaze quickly and efficiently taking her in before he turned his attention back to his son. "You didn't mention that you were bringing a guest."

Marcie could almost feel the irritation bristle through Chance's body when he placed his hand at the small of her back. His father had managed to make a simple statement sound like a criticism, an accusation of wrongdoing and a condemnation all in one breath. The little tickle of anxiety that had settled in her stomach as they'd driven up in front of the imposing house started to churn.

"I didn't think one more person would be noticed among all those already here. I trust you'll be able to stretch the food to accommodate one more place at the table." She heard the bitterness in his voice, but before his father could respond Chance quickly proceeded with introductions. "Marcie, this is my father...Douglas Fowler. Dad, this is Marcie Roper."

Douglas Fowler held out his hand, which Marcie accepted with a quick and efficient handshake. There was no warmth to his touch, nor was there any humanity. She quickly withdrew her hand.

He conveyed a practiced smoothness as he spoke. "It's nice to meet you, my dear. Now tell me...however did you and my son get together? You don't appear to be the type of woman he usually—''

''I had lost a package, dropped it on the street. Chance found it and was gracious enough to return it to me.'' She extended a pleasant smile even though his condescending manner sliced right through her like a hot knife through butter.

Her first reaction to him had been intimidation. But her second had been resentment at his attempt to belittle her. She knew that if she did not cut off his words right then and there, she would end up saying something she would later regret. The last thing she wanted was to embarrass Chance in front of his father.

''Come on, I'll show you around.'' Chance took command of the situation and escorted her inside, leaving his father standing at the front door.

The breath caught in Marcie's throat as she got her first glimpse past the entry hall. ''Oh, Chance...this is incredible. It looks like something from the cover of *Architectural Digest* magazine.''

''It's the best money can buy.'' There was

no mistaking the cynical overtones of his comment.

Marcie looked around the large living room with the cathedral ceilings. It had been lavishly decorated for Christmas, including a nine foot Christmas tree. It reeked of big money and prestige. Each individual item of holiday decoration had been meticulously placed so it enhanced the overall look and feel of the room without seeming to be out of place.

Sumptuous was the word that leaped to mind, followed by a quick jolt of inadequacy. This was a world she had never been part of, never even experienced. She had managed to shove the differences in hers and Chance's backgrounds aside, had convinced herself that it did not matter. But suddenly it loomed in front of her and was very real.

She swept her gaze across the room one more time. The look was impressive, but the feel was cold and impersonal. She could see another room beyond the living room. It appeared to be some sort of family room or den. There were several people in that room, both adults and children.

Chance leaned close to her as they walked through the living room and whispered in her ear, "Are you discouraged yet?" He tugged playfully at her earlobe with his lips. "Ready to turn and run?"

She was determined not to let her anxieties show. "Don't be silly. We just got here."

"All right, I've given you every opportunity. I guess there's nothing left to do except introduce you to the rest of the family."

She heard it in his voice—the lighthearted teasing that tried to mask the underlying layer of dread at the unavoidable. And she was beginning to understand his reticence. The surroundings were both beautiful and impressive, but it was a house rather than a real home. She did not feel any warmth or happiness. The walls did not radiate any love. It went a long way toward explaining Chance's cynical attitude where home and family were concerned.

He gave her a tour of the house, introduced her to aunts, uncles, cousins, and assorted other relatives and guests. There was the obligatory small talk prior to dinner. It felt to her as if she were under some sort of a microscope. Her discomfort increased with each passing minute and her feelings of inadequacy became more acute. She certainly knew the rules of etiquette for a formal meal and could carry on a conversation on a variety of topics, but that did not prevent her from being aware of how out of place she was in Chance's world.

It seemed to her as if everyone was studying her, silently judging her according to a set of rules known only to them. Questions directed her way sounded more like an inquisition than polite conversation. On more than one occasion Chance stepped in and terminated the conversation under the guise of showing her more of the house.

Finally all the guests were summoned—she did not know how else to interpret it other than a summons from on high—to the dining room for dinner. Douglas Fowler sat at the head of the table and presided over the gathering much in the same manner as a feudal lord over his fiefdom.

The meal and the surroundings may have been opulent, but the atmosphere was stark and austere. The dinner conversation seemed strained. The only moment of warmth occurred when Chance reached under the table and clasped her hand in his, giving it a little squeeze of reassurance.

After dinner everyone moved to the living

room where Douglas Fowler handed out professionally wrapped Christmas presents to all the children. Each child was prompted by a parent to make sure they properly thanked the patriarch for his generosity.

There was a pause in the festivities between the gift exchange for the children and the next scheduled event, which was the gift exchange for the adults. Chance took advantage of the lull in the proceedings to quietly escort Marcie out a side door before the adult portion of the evening's activities resumed.

His voice carried the full impact of the strain he felt. "I hope you're ready to leave, because I've had it."

Without waiting for an answer, he quickly ushered her to the car and a minute later they were passing through the gate at the end of the driveway. Neither of them spoke as he drove toward her house, Chance deep in thought and Marcie respecting his apparent need for the solitude. It was just as well. She felt the dull thud forming at her temples foretelling the onset of a headache directly attributable to the stresses of the day.

It had been one of the most unpleasant functions she had attended in a long time. The house had been filled with people who were there ostensibly to celebrate a time of togetherness with loved ones and family, but even the sounds of Christmas music filtering throughout the rooms could not alleviate the oppressive mood that hung heavily in the air. And the sheer magnitude of the surroundings had done nothing to lighten the mood for her. More than ever she felt the heavy weight of the differences between Chance and herself.

Chance pulled into Marcie's driveway. As soon as they were inside her house he grabbed her and pulled her body tight against his. He folded her into his embrace, demonstrating an almost frantic need to have her in his arms.

He caressed her shoulders, ran his fingers through the silky strands of her hair, and continued to hold her. A feeling of warmth and closeness finally settled over him, totally enveloping his senses and calming the strain in his tensed muscles. For the first time since they'd arrived at his father's house, he finally began to relax.

"Oh, Marcie..." He sighed her name as much as spoke it. His words were soft, coming from the very depths of his emotions. "I'm so sorry for subjecting you to what passes as holiday togetherness in my family. I had no right to drag you into what must have been an incredibly awkward situation for you.'' He released her just enough to cup her face in his hands. He placed a loving kiss on her lips, then plumbed the depth of her eyes. ''Thank you for going with me. You made the whole ridiculous charade bearable.''

''I'm glad I could help.'' She paused for a moment, not sure whether she should ask her question, but curiosity got the best of her. ''Tell me, does your family always put your dates through the wringer at your Christmas get-together the way they did me today?''

''No.''

She wrinkled her brow in confusion. ''You mean, I'm the first one who has ever been given the third degree?'' Had he only taken women from his own social stratum to his father's house? Was she the first *outsider* ever to grace the hallowed halls?

''No. I meant you're the only woman I've ever taken to the family Christmas dinner.''

His words both shocked and pleased her. She was the *only* woman he had ever taken to his father's house. Some of her anxieties began to lessen as his words settled over her consciousness.

Chance had never allowed anyone else to get so far inside him and his feelings as he had with Marcie Roper. He had never felt as comfortable with another human being as he did with her.

He took her hand in his and they walked down the hall to the bedroom. He was in desperate need of the feeling of closeness and caring that she provided. For the first time in his life Chance Fowler truly felt at one with someone and that person was Marcie Roper. His father had once again handed him another sobering dose of what marriage and family life were all about. He and Marcie did not need any of that. There was no reason for them to speak of commitment or what the future held. As far as he was concerned, things between them were perfect just as they were and there was no need for it to change.

Coy games were not part of their lovemaking. Pieces of clothing quickly fell away and moments later they snuggled together in the softness of her bed. She sensed his need for emotional closeness as much as the physical passion that existed between them. She openly responded to it by providing him with that comfort.

She held him in her arms as she gently stroked his broad shoulders and muscular back. He trailed his fingers over the smooth skin on her stomach, down her thighs, then across the swell of her breasts. He paused periodically to place a kiss at the base of her throat or behind her ear.

They shut out the world and, more specifically, the unpleasant memories of the afternoon and evening they had spent with Chance's family. They existed only for each other.

Gentle caresses eventually gave way to more urgent desires. A tingle of excitement raced through her body every time her fingers came in contact with his bare skin, only to be heightened by the sensation of his touch as he became more ardent in his zeal.

He captured her mouth in a heated kiss while rolling her body over on top of his. He tangled his fingers in her hair with one hand and ran his other hand across the delectable curve of her bottom. He twined his tongue with hers, reveling in the sensation of the texture. Her taste filled his senses, creating a demand for more. He knew that if he lived to be a hundred years old, he would never be able to get enough of her taste, her touch, the heat of her passion. He would always want more.

He broke off the kiss, nuzzling his face lower until he found the tautly puckered nipple. He drew the delectable treat into his mouth and began to suckle. The fires of his passion raced through his body.

She felt his rigid arousal pressing against her thigh. She shifted her weight slightly until her legs straddled his body. A moment later his hands were at her hips, raising her and then lowering her onto his hardened manhood. She felt the moan of pleasure leave her throat as he filled her to the depths. Once again they were joined together in an act of love that far surpassed anything she had known before Chance Fowler became part of her life.

He had unselfishly allowed her to set the rhythm and control of their lovemaking. One second she wanted to slowly savor each and every intimate moment and the next she wanted the fires of ecstasy to totally consume her.

Marcie excited him far beyond what he thought was possible and made him feel things he never knew existed—both physically and emotionally. He desperately needed to force some control over the way his passions were racing full speed ahead. He rolled her over onto her back and settled his body over hers. He established a new rhythm in hopes of prolonging their lovemaking.

He buried his face against her neck. His words came out thick and ragged. "You are absolutely breathtaking." He quickly captured her mouth with a hot kiss before he said more than he wanted to.

Their hips moved together in harmony, his downstroke meeting her upward thrust with an ever-increasing excitement. She felt the convulsions take hold then spread through her body. She tightened her legs around his hips and gave herself over totally to the intense sensations that reached to every corner of her reality.

The intensity built, then the spasms shuddered through Chance's body. He held her in his arms until the spasms quieted and he regained some control over his breathing. It was as if all the cares of the world had simply floated away, leaving him with only blissful happiness in the form of a woman wrapped in his loving embrace.

The afterglow of their lovemaking was a quiet time of gentle caresses and tender kisses. They were so comfortable with each other that neither felt the need to spoil the feeling of closeness with conversation. It was not very long before Marcie fell asleep in his arms. Chance, however, had too many things going through his mind for sleep to be able to take hold.

He had hoped Marcie would not pick up on the way his family had been subtly pumping her for information, but she had been too astute to miss it. He could see his father's fine hand behind the meddling. His anxiety over taking her to his father's house had been due in part to his concern about his father using it as an opportunity to pry into his private life. And that was precisely what had happened. He was not sure exactly what the outcome of his father's intrusion would be, but he knew it was not going to be to his benefit.

Marcie stirred in her sleep. Chance leaned over, kissed her softly on the forehead, then closed his eyes. He could not do anything about his father's interference tonight, so there was no point in losing any more sleep over it. He would tackle the problem in the morning. First thing in the morning he would...

He felt himself slipping over the edge into sleep before he could finish the thought. He pulled Marcie's body closer to his. Thoughts and feelings of love swirled around inside him, shoving everything else into the background.

Nine

Chance woke early the next morning. He gently shook Marcie's shoulder to wake her. She stretched, opened her eyes and focused on his face. A soft smile came to her lips and a feeling of warmth settled over her as she thought of waking up every morning with Chance next to her.

"I'm sorry to wake you so early, but I've got a rather busy day and I need to get going. I have a meeting first thing this morning with my stockbroker, then a luncheon meeting with my attorney—boring, but necessary." He placed a loving kiss on her forehead as he smoothed her mussed hair away from her face.

She sat up as she made an effort to suppress

a teasing grin. "Then you'd better get started. I wouldn't want to be responsible for keeping you here against your will."

He cupped her chin in his hand and looked into the depths of her eyes. His voice took on a seriousness that had not been there a moment earlier. "I don't seem to have much willpower where you're concerned. I don't know if that's good or bad."

Before she could respond to the heartfelt statement he climbed out of bed and reached for his clothes. He dressed quickly, then leaned over the bed and brushed a soft kiss across her lips. "I'll talk to you later."

Chance hurried out the door, got in his car, and drove down the street. He had not meant to say it, but it was true. He was in way over his head. Knowledge of what the consequences could be had always been frightening to him, but now the reality of how close they were at hand had him worried. As much as he tried to convince himself that things could go along just as they were, he knew it wasn't so. At some point he would have to make a commitment to Marcie and their relationship or else get out. He knew he could never voluntarily sever the connection, but would he ever be able to take that next step?

As soon as Marcie heard the front door close she got out of bed. She, too, had a busy day. Thoughts and images of the disastrous day spent with Chance's family kept coming back to her along with the need he had shown for the closeness of family that was missing from his life. Her Christmas holidays had been plagued by loneliness since her grandmother had died, but Chance's situation was almost brutal in the cold, impersonal feeling that surrounded the events of Sunday's gathering. She wished there was something she could do to make things better for him. It was a thought that remained with her as she started her workday.

Douglas Fowler pressed the intercom button and barked out an order. "Come in here."

A moment later Anne Metcalfe appeared in his office with pad and pencil, ready to take down his instructions. "Yes, Mr. Fowler. What do you need?"

"When you talked to my son, did he mention anything to you about bringing a young woman with him to Christmas dinner?"

"No, he didn't. He didn't say much of anything other than he'd note the date on his calendar. Is there a problem?"

His brow furrowed into a frown. "I don't know. This is the first time Chance has ever brought any of his women to the house. I interpret that to mean he is serious about this one. She lives in Crestview Bay and her name is Marcie Roper. She certainly does not come from an acceptable family background." His voice carried the full weight of his disdain for anything and anyone not of his self-determined social standing—a level of status he equated with money. "She works as a gardener, or something like that."

He leaned back in his chair and lit a cigar. "Get in touch with Roy McCaddan. She's obviously nothing more than a fortune hunter. Chance is so busy thinking with his libido that he can't see through her little game. Tell McCaddan I want an in-depth report on this woman on my desk no later than Thursday morning."

"Yes, Mr. Fowler. Right away." Anne returned to her office and immediately placed a call to Roy McCaddan, the head of security for Fowler Industries.

*   *   *

The day progressed smoothly for Marcie. She turned her attention to formulating her spring orders for specialty items the nursery would carry. That afternoon she went out to buy the little Christmas remembrances for her employees. They were nothing elaborate, just tokens of her appreciation. She had never referred to them as gifts because she did not want her employees to feel obligated to reciprocate.

Late afternoon she stopped by Chance's landscaping job to check on how things were progressing before returning to the nursery. She was surprised to see Chance's car at the cottage. She was even more surprised to see him dressed in worn jeans and an old T-shirt and up to his elbows in sawdust. Then she remembered Hank's words about Chance sometimes working alongside the construction crew, that he found it relaxing to get in and work with his hands.

She stood in the doorway watching him for a couple of minutes. The intense expression on his face showed signs of worry more so than a deep concentration on the physical work at hand. Something was obviously troubling him.

"Hi. This is a surprise finding you here."

Chance whirled around at the sound of her voice. The startled expression on his face quickly turned to pleasure. "Hi, yourself. I'll have to say that I'm equally surprised to find you here." He brushed at the sawdust on his clothes then wiped his hands on his T-shirt before putting his arm around her shoulder. "Is there a problem, or were you just in the neighborhood?"

"Just in the neighborhood. How about you? I thought you had meetings all day."

"No, only half the day."

She placed her hand against his chest and looked up at his face. His expression had become pensive and he seemed to be staring out the window without really focusing on anything. A little tremor of apprehension flickered inside her. "Is there something wrong?"

He jerked his attention back to her as he forced a smile. "No, nothing's wrong." He leaned over and placed a quick kiss on her forehead. "I was just thinking about what else needed to be done with this staircase now that the paint has been stripped and the rough spots sanded." The staircase was not the only thing on his mind. He was also contemplating his problem. Working with his hands, doing the physical labor, helped him clear his mind so that he could think through his problems.

Problem—he knew it was a poor choice of words when referring to his relationship with the woman he loved. He seemed to be getting more confused by the moment. Marcie was the most wonderful person in the world, yet he could not force out the words to tell her how much he loved her.

"I was going to stop by the nursery at closing time. Do you have any plans for tonight? I thought we might do something together."

"I have an appointment with a client in La Jolla this evening. They're adding a conservatory to their house and we're going to provide all the plants."

"Sounds like a big project."

"It is, and I'm real excited about it. It's going to be quite a showplace when it's finished."

Marcie stayed for a few minutes longer, then continued on her way. Chance might have thought he'd covered his true thoughts and feelings, but he had not fooled her for a minute. She knew something was wrong and she knew exactly what the something was—he was still upset about the Christmas dinner at his father's house and felt badly about her not having a good time.

It had been late when Marcie returned home from her meeting. She found an outrageous message from Chance on her answering machine making erotic suggestions, then wishing her pleasant dreams. Once again the warm feeling of love she felt for him settled over her. She went straight to bed and immediately fell asleep, not stirring until she woke the next morning.

The day turned out to be equally as busy as the day before had been. In addition to the normal duties of her workday, Marcie had one thought that kept circulating through her mind—she wanted to make this Christmas one of love and closeness, a time for happiness and giving. She had seen what Chance's Christmas was like and she knew of the unsettled loneliness of her own life during the holiday season since her grandmother's death. This year would be different. She had found a man to whom she could give her heart and her love. She would see to it that the unpleasant day spent at his father's house was a thing of the past.

Her company Christmas party was just a few days away. She would make sure that it was the best party they ever had. As her time allowed during the day she made a list of everything she needed to buy and gathered some additional Christmas items from the nursery inventory. On her way home from work she stopped and made her purchases. This would be the old-fashioned Christmas she had always dreamed of, filled with love and caring. For the first time in more years than she could remember, she looked forward to the holidays.

And it was all because of Chance Fowler.

She juggled her packages in her hands as she unlocked her front door. A few minutes later everything lay spread out across the living room floor. She looked around at the minimal amount of decorating she had already done in preparation for the company party. It was, indeed, sparse and uninspiring. She set about unwrapping her purchases. Before she could finish, the phone rang.

"Hello?"

"So, you finally got home from work." Chance's voice teased, immediately eliminating any sense of accusation his words might have carried. "I tried to call several times, but no one answered."

A soft warm glow spread through her body as soon as she heard his voice. "I stopped to do some shopping and the time got away from me. I didn't realize how late it was."

"Is it too late for company?"

"Well..." She hesitated a moment. If he was calling from his house then it would take him a while to get to her house and it was already going on nine o'clock. "Where are you?"

"I'm just turning the corner at the end of your block."

A moment later she saw the headlights of a car pulling into her driveway. She carried her cordless phone to the front door and peered out. She saw Chance climb out of his car with his cellular phone in his hand.

Marcie opened the door as the amused grin curled the corners of her mouth. "Do you suppose it would be okay if we hang up and talk face-to-face or do you want to continue this conversation at however much money you're being charged per minute for your cell phone?'' She pushed the off button on her phone to disconnect the call.

Chance placed his cellular phone and his car keys on her dining room table, then turned and pulled her into his arms. ''I think face-to-face is a much nicer concept. It's so much more *personal.*'' He brushed a soft kiss on her lips before letting her go.

''You drove from San Diego to Crestview Bay when you knew I wasn't home?'' She flashed him a teasing grin. ''Or did you just happen to be in the neighborhood and thought you'd stop by?''

''After the second time of calling and not getting your answering machine, I began to worry.'' As if to validate his words, a look of concern darted across his features, but he quickly covered it.

''Oh, I see.'' She rested her head against his shoulder when he pulled her into his embrace. ''So you just thought you'd jump in your car and take a drive out this way because you didn't have anything better to do with your time.''

''Something like that.'' He placed a soft kiss on her forehead. ''Actually, it was your answering machine.''

She looked up at the genuine concern that blanketed his features again. "My answering machine? What about it?"

"I couldn't figure out why you would have gone out and not turned on your answering machine." He admitted to himself that it sounded rather silly now, but he had been genuinely worried. It was not that he needed to know where she was, it was just that she had obviously intended to be home or her answering machine would have been on. Either she had turned it off then left again or something else had happened. The thought of her being harmed in any way had truly upset him.

She chuckled as she wiggled out of his embrace and went to the kitchen. "Is that all? The truth is, I never turned it on before leaving for work this morning." She took two glasses from the cupboard and filled them with ice tea from the refrigerator. "And it's all your fault, too."

"My fault?"

"You left me that message telling me to have pleasant dreams...so I did. In fact, they were so pleasant that I overslept this morning and ended up rushing out the door. By the time

I remembered that I hadn't turned on the machine I was already at work."

He backed her up against the kitchen counter and pressed his body against hers. "I guess I have no option. I accept the blame." He toyed with the top button on her blouse, slowly unfastening it as he whispered in her ear, "I'll see if I can make it up to you." He captured her mouth with a tantalizing sensuality.

His kiss filled her with warmth and caring. Every time he touched her he lit an intense fire under her desires, but that was lust and with time it would begin to diminish. The warmth and caring—that was the type of loving feeling that lasted a lifetime.

He unfastened the second button on her blouse. His lips were so close to hers that she could feel his words as well as hear them. "You have quite a pile of stuff on the living room floor. Is that something you plan to do tonight—" The third button of her blouse gave way under the manipulation of his nimble fingers. "Or can we concentrate on more interesting things? Like this..." He leaned down and kissed the notch at the base of her throat. "And maybe this..." He ran the tip of his tongue across the swell of her breast, tracing along the edge of her bra.

She closed her eyes and leaned her head back as the smile of contentment curled at the corners of her mouth. "Hmm... You do present an intriguing and very persuasive argument."

She allowed his half-teasing and half-serious seduction to continue for a moment longer before bringing it to a halt. She placed her hand against his chest and applied just enough pressure so he'd know that she wanted him to stop. "However, before we reach the point of no return, I do have things that need to be done this evening. Since you're here, do you suppose I could talk you into giving me a hand? It kind of involves you, anyway."

A mischievous twinkle lit up his eyes and a sly grin tugged at the corners of his mouth. "And just what do I get in exchange for all this magnificent help I'm going to provide?"

She returned his teasing manner. "How about a feeling of satisfaction at a job well done?"

"Is that the best offer you have?"

She reached her face up to his, brushing a

tender kiss across his lips. ''That's the only offer I have.''

''You're a tough negotiator, Marcie Roper. You leave me no option other than to accept your terms.''

He picked up the two glasses of ice tea, handed one of them to her, then escorted her to the living room. ''So tell me, what kind of work detail is this?''

''It's Christmas.'' She saw the blank look cross his face. ''As you know, this coming Monday is my annual company Christmas party that you agreed to attend. I've invited Hank Varney and your construction crew in addition to my employees and select clients.''

She set her glass on the coffee table and began opening packages. ''I bought a whole bunch of new Christmas decorations. I want to decorate my house like never before. I want this to be the best Christmas party ever.''

He saw the enthusiasm radiate from her face and heard it in her voice. She had caught him totally off guard. He had thought that the disaster at his father's house would have put a permanent damper on any Christmas spirit. That was what it had done to him. But now, seeing and hearing her sudden burst of excitement, he could not help but be caught up in it. They could spend Christmas together. It would be the first meaningful Christmas of his adult life.

The grin spread across his face until it became a dazzling smile. "Okay. If decorating is what you want to do, then decorating is what we'll do." He picked up one of the packages while staring at the others. "What all do you have here?"

They worked for three hours, totally absorbed in the task at hand. Some of her existing decorations were taken down and packed away to be replaced with new items. Other purchases were carefully placed, studied, moved, studied again, and finally given the perfect spot. They weren't quite finished when the clock chimed midnight and reminded them how late it was.

Marcie surveyed their work and was pleased with how much they had accomplished. She turned to Chance. "What do you think? Is it shaping up okay? Do you think it will look good for the party?"

"I think it will look terrific." She seemed to bubble with effervescence. The excitement in her voice and the sparkle in her eyes proved to be a heady combination that was more contagious than he had anticipated. Before he knew what was happening, that same ebullience bubbled up inside him. He felt almost like a kid again as the prospect of a warm and close holiday loomed on the horizon, clearly within his reach. It was going to be a memorable Christmas—a Christmas filled with love. And there was nothing that could spoil it. A dark thought tried to work its way into his consciousness but he refused to allow it.

"I'm going to get the Christmas tree tomorrow and finish the decorating tomorrow night."

He nuzzled his face into her neck. "Am I to assume that you'll require my services to finish this job?"

"The job isn't done yet." She ran her hands up under his sweater and stroked her fingers across his bare back. "I expect you to finish what you start."

He caressed her shoulders, ran his hands down her back, and finally cupped the roundness of her bottom in his hands. He pulled her hips tight against his and brushed a soft kiss against her mouth. "I wouldn't want anyone to accuse me of not finishing what I started."

He lifted her into his arms and carried her toward the bedroom.

All day long little twinges of excitement kept tickling through Marcie's body. This was going to be the best Christmas ever. She selected the perfect Christmas tree from among those that she had for sale, a six-foot noble fir, and set it aside. "Glen, would you have Don drop this tree off at my house when he makes his deliveries this afternoon?"

He inspected the tree, then shot her a teasing grin. "This is a nice tree. Does it mean you've finally given up on that artificial tree you've been using since before time began?"

She returned his grin with one of her own. "You sound like someone who doesn't want a Christmas bonus this year."

He immediately straightened to attention and gave her a snappy salute. "Yes, ma'am. It'll be done just as soon as Don finishes replanting those ficus trees in five-gallon containers." He carried the fir tree out the back door toward the delivery truck.

The balance of the afternoon went quickly. Marcie stopped at the grocery store after leaving work for the day. With each passing hour the excitement inside her bubbled closer and closer to the surface. She could not wait to see Chance, to see his reaction to her decision about the Christmas tree decorations.

As soon as she arrived home she rushed to get things started. She took out a large bowl and immediately began popping the bags of microwave popcorn, one after the other, until she had filled the bowl. She found another large bowl, then put the next popcorn bag into the microwave just as the doorbell rang.

Marcie rushed to the door, knowing it was Chance. "Hi."

Chance immediately noticed the noble fir standing by the front window. "So this is the kind of tree you decided on." He walked over and inspected it. "These are pretty expensive, but they are so unusual looking. I'm sure it will look great after it's decorated."

"I was hoping to have everything ready before you got here so that we could start right away, but I had to stop at the store on the way home. I had planned to do it on my way to work, but didn't have enough time."

"Oh? What happened?" His voice dripped with the same feigned innocence that covered his features. "Did you oversleep?" He put his arm around her shoulder and walked with her to the kitchen.

"Not exactly. If you recall, you wouldn't let me out of bed this morning. By the time I got you out the door I had to rush to get to work on time."

Chance dropped his voice to a low, seductive whisper. "You didn't seem to have any complaints about it this morning."

She purred softly in his ear. "You know what mercurial creatures we women are. That was then and this is now. You had me so befuddled this morning that I didn't realize how late it was."

"I only had you befuddled? That's not very flattering. I was trying for much more than simply befuddled."

Her words were a mere whisper. "And you succeeded."

It was a tender moment as he held her in his arms. She rested her head against his shoulder and he settled his cheek against her head. They stood together, wrapped in each other's embrace for a full minute before Chance raised his head.

"Is that popcorn I smell?"

"It certainly is. I also bought cranberries. I

want to decorate the tree with lots and lots of popcorn and cranberry garlands, and old-fashioned ornaments.''

''Uh-oh, this sounds like work. I get the impression that you think we're going to string all of that popcorn and those cranberries.''

''Yep...that's exactly what I had in mind. I thought you could build a fire in the fireplace and I'd put these Christmas CDs in the player to set the mood, and we'd get to work.''

Neither of them had realized exactly how much work stringing popcorn was and how much time it took. They laughed and talked as they worked—one piece of popcorn for the garland, one piece of popcorn in the mouth. They ended up eating as much popcorn as they made into garlands. At one point during the evening Chance had to make a trip to the grocery store to buy more popcorn.

They made some garlands of popcorn only, others consisting of only cranberries, and some that alternated the popcorn with the cranberries. It was almost one o'clock in the morning when they finished making the strands and they still had not put one single decoration on the tree yet.

''As much as I don't like the idea—'' he

paused as he brushed his fingertips longingly across her cheek "—I need to go. I have an early-morning appointment close to my house."

Marcie tried to stifle a yawn without much success. "If I'd known how long this was going to take, I wouldn't have suggested it."

Chance held her hand as they walked toward the front door. "I'm glad you did." He pulled her into his embrace as he leaned against the doorjamb. "I wouldn't have missed this for anything." He brushed a soft kiss against her lips. "Thank you. For the first time in many years, I think this will be a Christmas to remember."

Marcie watched as Chance drove away. A warm feeling of satisfaction settled deep inside her. She, too, felt the same way. This was going to be a Christmas to remember. She locked the door, turned out the living room lights, and retreated to her bedroom. It had been a very long day and she was dead tired.

Chance glanced back at Marcie's house as he drove down the street. He saw the living room windows go dark, then the light come on in her bedroom.

There was only one thing that could spoil the wonderful feeling of contentment that had been with him for the entire evening. And, unfortunately, that one thing would be the first item on his agenda in the morning. He had an appointment with his father—at his father's *request,* which in itself was very strange.

Douglas Fowler did not make requests, he issued orders. Chance did not know what his father wanted, but Anne Metcalfe had inquired about his availability. His father did not normally care about anyone else's schedule—his time was important, not any one else's. He simply summoned people when he wanted them. But this time he had made a request and the implications had Chance worried.

Ten

———

"It's nice to see you, Chance." Douglas Fowler indicated a chair for his son, then took his place behind the large mahogany desk. "I'm glad you were able to join us last Sunday...you and your *friend.*"

Chance's insides twisted into a hard knot. So that was it. His father was about to pry into his relationship with Marcie. Well, it would do him no good. They had nothing to discuss.

"Could we get to whatever it is that's on your mind and skip all the meaningless little pleasantries? I have a busy schedule today and need to get going."

"Very well." Douglas Fowler opened a file folder and picked up a sheet of paper. "I have here a report on your little friend, Marcie Roper. She comes from a middle-class economic background. Her family tree is totally uninspired with not even one notable member to help elevate her status. I do show that she has a college degree, but it's nothing more than a Bachelor of Liberal Arts from a small community college. I see fortune hunter written all over this.''

''Fortune hunter!'' Chance's anger propelled him out of the chair like a shot. ''That's what this is about?'' He spit out the words before he could stop himself. He felt the anger contort his features. He clenched his jaw in an attempt to push it aside. The last thing he wanted to do was lose his cool in front of his father. He did not want to give his father the satisfaction of seeing that he had gotten to him. He took a deep breath, held it for a moment, then exhaled.

Chance spoke slowly and succinctly, so there could be no misunderstanding as to what he said and exactly what he meant. ''By no stretch of anyone's imagination is Marcie Roper a fortune hunter.'' He heard the sharp edge to his voice and made no attempt to hide it. ''She's an independent, self-reliant woman.

She owns her own business and works hard at making it a success. I thoroughly resent the fact that you had her investigated.''

He leaned forward in an aggressive manner, placing the palms of his hands flatly against the top of his father's desk. He fixed the elder Fowler with a hard stare. ''Who she is and what type of relationship we have is absolutely none of your business.'' He straightened, but did not relinquish his aggressive manner.

Douglas Fowler took his time snipping the end of his cigar and lighting it, purposely dragging out the action so that Chance would have to wait until he was ready to continue the conversation. It was a tactic Chance had seen his father use on many occasions and he was not going to allow himself to be manipulated by it.

''You can play your little mind games and use your stalling tactics on someone else because I'm not interested. Whenever you're ready to get around to the real purpose of this little meeting, let me know. In fact, why don't you send me an e-mail and save both of us the aggravation of another confrontation.'' Chance abruptly turned on his heel and started toward the door.

Douglas Fowler's authoritative voice boomed across the office. ''Don't you walk out on me while I'm talking to you. Get back here now or I'll—''

Chance whirled around and glared at his father. ''Or you'll what? Send me to bed without any dinner? Make me stand in the corner? Cut off my allowance? I'm not a child and I resent your attempt to treat me as such. Maybe I need to remind you that you don't give me an allowance.''

''Calm down, Chance. I only have your best interests in mind. One day all of this will be yours. I want to protect your inheritance.''

''Humph! Concern over my inheritance— that would be a real touching speech if there was even the slightest bit of truth to it. Regardless of what the newspapers say and what people think, I'm not the spoiled playboy who lives off his father's indulgence. I do quite nicely without any financial assistance from you.''

''Yes. Your mother and her father saw to that.''

''Well, thank you for the vote of confidence. Yes, there was a small trust fund that came to me on my twenty-first birthday. But I'm the one who built it into a sizable amount that pays me enough money to take care of my needs, and I did that without any help from you. I'm the one who finances the construction schools, not you.''

Douglas Fowler backed off a little from his domineering manner, but did not lose his assertive attitude. "It seems that every time we try to have a conversation it ends up in an argument. It would be nice if one time we could just talk.''

"The word conversation implies a back-and-forth exchange. You don't know how to have a conversation—to *just talk*. You give orders and expect everyone to jump at your commands. Unlike your employees and probably a significant number of your clients and business associates, I'm not afraid of your power or your money. As to that charming little family get-together last Sunday, it will probably be my last appearance. And as for Marcie Roper—'' He could not stop the angry scowl that covered his face. "You leave her alone.'' His words were pointed and left no confusion about their meaning.

Chance exited the office without waiting for a response, but not before noting with some satisfaction the stunned expression on his father's face.

As soon as Chance closed the outer office door, Douglas Fowler punched the intercom and snapped out his command to Anne Metcalfe. "Get George Dunlop on the phone."

A minute later Anne buzzed him to pick up the phone.

"George, I want you to draw up a document for me. I want to see a rough draft of it by next Tuesday."

Douglas Fowler issued his specific instructions and quickly concluded his conversation with his attorney. He leaned back in his large leather chair and lit his cigar.

Chance hurried from his father's office to the parking garage to reclaim his car. The anger still churned in the pit of his stomach. The nagging concern that had pricked at his consciousness for the past few days had proved to be correct. He never should have subjected Marcie to the Sunday get-together, never should have allowed his father to know she even existed. He took a calming breath. He had made his feelings perfectly clear to his father.

That should be the end of it...at least he hoped so.

He turned his attention toward more pleasant thoughts, ones that filled him with warmth and contentment—an old-fashioned evening of stringing popcorn and listening to Christmas music, the joy of putting up decorations and preparing for a party, a house filled with happy people enjoying themselves and the company of their friends. And spending Christmas eve with a beautiful woman who meant more to him than anything in the world. It was something that had never before been part of his life and he was looking forward to embracing it wholeheartedly.

The day passed quickly for Marcie and Chance as they each took care of business matters. That evening he returned to her house to help her finish the Christmas decorating.

Chance stood on the small ladder and hung the last of the ornaments on the upper branches of the tree. ''How does that look?''

Marcie scrunched up her nose while studying the symmetry of the arrangement. He changed the position of three of the ornaments in response to her negative expression.

''Does this look better?''

She stared at it for a moment. "Let me see it back the first way you had it."

He made the changes as she requested, then climbed off the ladder and stood next to her. "Well? What do you think?"

She turned a beaming smile toward him. "I think it looks perfect. In fact, I think it's the most beautiful tree I've ever seen. How about you?"

His words were soft and so very sincere. "I think *you* are the most beautiful thing *I've* ever seen." He placed a kiss on the tip of her nose, then quickly reverted back to an upbeat manner. "But as far as Christmas trees go, I think you're right...this is definitely of prize-winning caliber."

She went to the front door and stood with her back to it, looking into the living room and beyond to the dining room. She reflected on the results of their decorating efforts. She spoke as much to herself as to him. "It really does look nice. It's warm, inviting, and cozy...just the type of place I've always—"

He put his arm around her shoulder as he, too, surveyed the transformation of living room and dining room into a festive holiday setting. "It's just the type of place where anyone would feel very comfortable spending Christmas.''

She looked up at him, her eyes seeking the truth of his approval and the reassurance of his words. She slipped her arm around his waist. ''Do you really think so? This is going to be a very special Christmas. I want everything to be perfect.''

''I'd say decoration-wise you're ready for your company party on Monday. Now, what do you plan to do about food and drink?''

''What I plan to do is spend all day Sunday cooking and Monday putting on the finishing touches. As far as drink is concerned, I'm going to have a large bowl of punch, soft drinks, coffee and tea, beer and wine. I think that should do it.''

''Sounds like more than enough to me. I'll tell you what...I'll buy the soft drinks, beer and wine.''

She pulled back from him, feigning an irritation at his suggestion. ''You're an invited guest, and more than that, you're a client of the landscaping service. I don't ask my customers to bring their own refreshments.''

He fixed her with a teasing glint in his eyes and a mischievous grin. ''I thought I was a little more than merely a customer.'' He pulled her into his arms and flicked the tip of his tongue along her lower lip, then whispered in her ear, ''Or is this the way you behave with all your business associates?''

She patted him affectionately on the rear as she extended a teasing grin. ''I'm not so sure that it's any of your business.'' The truth was that she had never behaved with anyone the way she did with Chance Fowler. She had never been so open…or so brazen.

They made a few minor changes to the decorations, then Marcie declared the job done. She was very pleased with the results. She glanced at her watch. ''Once again, it's very late. I'm not going into the nursery Saturday or Sunday unless someone calls me with an emergency. That means I'll have to work twice as hard tomorrow to make sure all my business matters are taken care of ahead of time.''

''I've got a busy day tomorrow, too. First thing in the morning I'm flying up to San Francisco to look at more property. I'll be staying overnight and should be back late Saturday afternoon. I was going to ask you to go with me, but it sounds like you won't have the time.…'' He allowed his voice to trail off, then added hopefully, "Or would you? I'd help you get ready for the party."

"No. As much as I'd like to, there's no way I can take the time."

"I'm going to miss you."

An amused grin tugged at the corners of her mouth. "I'll miss you, too."

He cupped her chin in his hand. His voice dropped to a whisper. "I mean, I'm *really* going to miss you."

"Your house looks great. I love all your decorations." Sandy's enthusiasm surrounded her words, just as it did with everything. "I think this is the best company Christmas party we've ever had." She poured herself a glass of punch and crossed the room to speak with some of the flower shop clients.

Marcie stood in the kitchen door and scanned the room with a critical eye. She had been a nervous wreck all day. This was without a doubt the most lavish company party she had ever attempted. It fact, it was the most lavish party of any type that she had ever planned. And it was also a bit of an eclectic mix of people. She began to relax a little when it became apparent that everyone was having a good time.

She had noticed earlier that Eric Ross had introduced Bob from Chance's construction crew to Glen, and now Glen and Bob seemed to be engaged in serious conversation. She hoped it would work out and Glen would be happy with Bob so she could hire him as the new nursery employee.

"You look a little stressed. Is everything okay?"

Marcie's head snapped up at the sound of Chance's voice. An embarrassed smile curved her lips slightly at the corners. "I thought I was doing a pretty good job of hiding it. Was I that obvious?"

"I'm sure no one else noticed." He touched his fingertip to the corner of her mouth and edged it up. "Come on, let's see that smile of yours, otherwise your guests will think you're not enjoying yourself."

She forced a full smile. "I'll try. I'm always nervous when it comes to entertaining in my home. I haven't had much experience at it and I'm always afraid I'll do something stupid." It was the first time she had ever admitted that to anyone. Chance made her feel so comfortable and special that nothing seemed too personal to admit.

He flashed an encouraging smile and gave her hand a confident squeeze. "The house looks terrific, the food tastes great, everyone is having a good time. There's nothing for you to worry about. Relax and join in the fun."

She looked around the room again. "I guess you're right."

He tugged at her hand. "Come on, let's dance. If we start, then I'm sure other people will join in."

Chance led her out to the patio, which had been decorated with colorful party lights. The weather had cooperated, the unseasonably warm temperature making for a beautiful night. He pulled her into his arms and moved with the music. Before long, other couples joined them on the patio, everyone moving to the sweet sounds that floated on the clear night air.

Marcie handed out her remembrances to her employees and everyone ended up singing Christmas carols. Even though the next morning was another workday, no one wanted to leave. They all declared the party to be a great success. It was almost midnight when the last guest finally departed.

"Whew! I'm glad that's over." Marcie leaned back against the front door and closed her eyes as she breathed a sigh of relief. "I'm exhausted." She opened her eyes and surveyed the aftermath. "From the look of things, I'd say everyone must have enjoyed themselves."

"It was a terrific party and everyone had a great time." Chance grabbed a large trash bag from the kitchen and began filling it with crumpled paper napkins, dirty paper plates and plastic forks.

A sudden jolt of inadequacy ricocheted through her body. Paper plates and plastic forks...there certainly had not been anything like that at Douglas Fowler's house. Nor, she was sure, would Chance ever serve his guests on paper and plastic. Had he been embarrassed by what he must have perceived as her lack of social graces? She had always thought she knew the proper thing to do and say in formal social situations, not that her party was really something *formal*, but did she really measure up to the standards he was accustomed to? Had she embarrassed him at his father's house in front of all his family members?

She was so head-over-heels in love with him that she had managed to shove aside her concerns about their vastly different backgrounds and life-styles. Perhaps doing so had been a major error on her part.

"Do you really think so? You're not just saying that, are you?" An almost timid apprehension covered her as her insecurities began to seep through. "It was the most elaborate party I've ever given, also the largest one. I've been a nervous wreck all evening."

He stopped what he was doing, reached out and took her hand in his, and pulled her to him. An amused chuckle made its way out into the open. "You know something? For someone who is so capable and self-sufficient, you sounded for a moment there as if you'd never given a dinner party before. Everything was marvelous."

She heard his words of praise, but how sincere were they? The hesitation still clung to her words. "Technically it wasn't a dinner party. It was just some snacks and drinks."

He put his arms around her. The concern on her face over such a simple thing touched his heart. "Well, whatever you want to call it, I can assure you that everyone had a great time.'' He held her for a moment as he mulled something over in his mind.

''Marcie...'' His voice trailed off. He was not sure about what he had in mind. He took a calming breath. This whole concept of the holidays being a time of joy was something new to him. He was not sure exactly how far to trust this new feeling.

''Yes?''

''There's, uh, there's a dance at the yacht club this weekend. Would you like to go?''

She looked up at him. ''The yacht club?'' She flashed on the image of the peacock blue evening gown and the red silk cocktail dress that she had been admiring in the store window the morning Chance Fowler burst into her life. ''Is it a formal affair or just a casual dance?''

''It's the annual Christmas dinner dance. To tell you truthfully, I've never gone to it before, so I don't know if it's tuxedo formal or just suit-and-tie dressy.''

Either way, it did not matter. ''I—I'm afraid I don't have anything appropriate to wear to such an occasion.''

She had been correct. He was yacht club and she was backyard barbecue. She looked around at the remnants of her party. Her paper plates and plastic forks suddenly seemed very shabby. What she thought was a festive yet comfortably decorated living room now seemed woefully inadequate when compared to the lavish decorations at his father's house and the type of setting the yacht club would present.

"Having something appropriate to wear is not a problem. Would you like to go?"

She took a couple of steps away from him. She suddenly felt very uncomfortable with who he was and what he represented.

"I don't know. I...well, to tell you truthfully, I've never been to a yacht club or a country club." She glanced awkwardly at the floor as the discomfort welled inside her. "I'm afraid I'd be out of place."

He lifted her chin with his fingertips. "You could never be out of place no matter where you went." He pulled her back into his arms and covered her mouth with a loving kiss.

Marcie stared at the wall calendar at the nursery. The yacht club dinner dance was that Saturday. She could not imagine what insanity had prompted her to accept Chance's invitation, other than his very persuasive technique of kissing her until her toes curled and she couldn't get her breath. She had no business at a yacht club dinner dance. She had nothing in common with any of those people.

An inadvertent little chuckle escaped into the open. As Chance had so succinctly reminded her when she voiced that exact concern, he was one of "those people" and the two of them certainly had lots of things in common.

She checked her schedule. The next day seemed to be a light workload. She would drive into San Diego first thing in the morning and go shopping for an appropriate dress to wear. Of course, that meant she would also have to buy a pair of shoes to match, and some type of appropriate wrap. A little twinge of anxiety knotted in the pit of her stomach. It was a lot of money to spend for something she would probably wear only once.

Her next thought came out of the clear blue. It was like a wedding gown...a lot of money to spend for something you only wear one time. A little hint of sadness invaded her thoughts. Or in her case, something it looked as if she would never have occasion to wear. She refused to allow that line of thought to continue. She would not speculate on the exact nature of her relationship with Chance Fowler or where it was headed…if anywhere at all. They were lovers, but was that all it would ever be? She heaved a heavy sigh and returned her attention to the advertising form from the phone company. She needed to renew her business ads in the phone book's Yellow Pages.

The rest of the day remained busy for her. That evening she and Chance went to a movie. What had started out as seeing each other about twice a week had become an almost daily occurrence. With the exception of when he was out of town or when she had evening appointments, they spent each night together. During the week they would be at her house. On weekends, when she did not have to go to work the next morning, they would be at his house.

When they were together, all the cares of the world simply disappeared for her. But when they were not together she worried about the future, their future together and whether or not they would even have one. She loved him so very much. Was it possible to love someone too much?

She was well acquainted with his negative

views on marriage and home life. He had made those opinions perfectly clear when they had first met. She knew that making a commitment to an ongoing relationship was not part of his personal philosophy. She thought she could live with that and had entered into the relationship with her eyes wide open to that possibility and the consequences. But now she was not so sure. It left her with a very unsettled feeling to not know where they were headed or even exactly how things stood between them. Yet she was reluctant to ask him about it for fear it might drive him away.

She shoved her doubts and concerns aside. This was an area where they simply did not see eye-to-eye and probably never would. She was a mature woman who knew exactly where he stood on commitment and what she was getting into. She had just never guessed exactly where it would end up taking her.

The next morning Marcie took care of her shopping. After trying on what seemed like dozens of dresses she finally settled on a red dress very similar to the one she had seen in the store window that fateful morning. She purchased shoes and the other accessories she needed to go with the dress, then hurried back to Crestview Bay.

A little tingle of excitement accompanied the packages as she carried them into her house. To her surprise she found that she was looking forward to the yacht club dinner dance. After all, Chance would not have invited her if he thought she would be out of place. She paused for a moment as a little tremor of anxiety tried to take hold. At least she hoped that was true.

The rest of the week seemed to fly by and before Marcie was ready for it, the day of the dinner dance had arrived. She had offered to drive to San Diego and meet Chance at his house to save him the trip to Crestview Bay, but he had insisted on picking her up. She glanced at the clock. Five-fifteen—Chance was due at five-thirty. She was almost ready. She sprayed a hint of perfume, put on her earrings, then slipped her feet into her shoes. She did a final check of her appearance in the full-length mirror just as the doorbell rang.

"You look gorgeous!" Chance closed the door behind him as he stepped into the living room. The sexy fragrance of her perfume tickled his senses. He took her hand in his. "In fact, you look far too delicious to waste on the yacht club crowd. What would you say to skipping the dinner dance and just staying in tonight?''

There was no mistaking the lascivious twinkle in his eye or the lecherous tone in his voice. She picked up her wrap and handed it to him. ''If you think I tried on every dress in San Diego and then spent the entire afternoon getting ready just to stay home, then you have another think coming.''

He helped her with her wrap. ''Then I guess we're off to the ball. Your carriage awaits.''

The butterflies continued to flit around inside her stomach as they drove from Crestview Bay to San Diego. It was the uncertainty of whether or not she could comfortably fit in with Chance's group of yacht club friends that caused her apprehension. Regardless of how many times he tried to reassure her and tell her she had no reason to worry, she could not keep the trepidation away. Her anxiety level increased as they pulled into the parking lot.

Marcie took a calming breath as Chance went around the car to open the door for her. He held out his hand to help her out. When she felt the warmth of his touch and the little squeeze he gave her hand, she knew everything would be all right.

Before they could even get to the front door there was a succession of flashes as a photographer clicked off a series of pictures of them. Chance immediately positioned himself between the photographer and Marcie, shielding her from the camera's view as much as possible. He clenched his jaw in a hard line and mumbled under his breath, "Damn photographers." He quickly ushered her inside the building.

"I'm sorry about that, Marcie. It didn't occur to me that someone would be here grabbing candid shots. I hope that didn't upset you too much." He gave her hand a little squeeze to reassure her.

"It was a little disconcerting, but no harm done." It was an odd sensation, being the subject of a roving photographer. This was the first time they had gone anywhere together that was this public. Being together at little out-of-the-way restaurants and the occasional movie had not attracted any photographers, but a Christmas dinner dance at the yacht club was obviously a different matter. They were in Chance's world now, not hers.

They arrived at the dining room and were immediately seated at their table. Marcie looked around, taking in everything. The room was lavishly decorated and the guests elegantly attired. Her gaze fell on Chance, seated across the table from her. He looked very handsome in his tuxedo. She glanced down at her own attire, as if to validate her choice of clothes. She was pleased with her decision to buy the red cocktail dress.

Chance ordered champagne, then they made their dinner selections. They had eyes only for each other as they ate. Afterward they danced to the music of the live orchestra until one o'clock in the morning. They were again assaulted by photographers as they left.

Chance headed the car toward his house. He reached over and took her hand. There was a hint of nervousness to his voice. "That wasn't so bad, was it?"

She paused a moment before offering a reply. "No, it wasn't." She had enjoyed the evening after getting over her initial resistance. "In fact, I had a very nice time in spite of the photographers."

"You sound surprised."

"I do have one complaint, though."

His brow furrowed for a moment. Not sure of what she was going to say, his nervousness resurfaced. "What's that?"

"My feet hurt."

His spontaneous laugh filled the car. "As soon as we get home I'll rub them for you. How's that?"

She leaned her head against his shoulder and closed her eyes as she stifled a yawn. "That sounds perfect."

Eleven

Monday turned out to be an unusually busy day for Marcie. With Christmas Eve coming up that Thursday, the flower shop was swamped and she ended up helping Sandy with the additional workload. It was a little after three in the afternoon when the well-dressed man in his late fifties made an appearance.

"Miss Roper?"

"Yes, I'm Marcie Roper."

"My name is George Dunlop." He handed her his business card.

"What can I do for you—" Marcie glanced at the card, then returned her attention to the stranger. "Mr. Dunlop?"

"I am the Fowler family attorney and am representing the interests of Chance Fowler. I have a document here—" he reached into his attaché case and produced a file folder "—that I've been instructed to give you."

Her brow wrinkled in confusion as she took the folder from him. Chance's attorney had something for her? Why had he not said something to her himself? He had mentioned having a meeting with his attorney and stockbroker the previous week. Could this be what his meeting was about? A moment of confusion and uncertainty welled inside her. Having his attorney contact her seemed so formal...and so impersonal.

"As you can see, there are three copies of said document. If you would just sign all three copies where indicated and return them to me, I will have a fully executed copy returned to you for your files."

She opened the folder and removed the top copy of the document. She glanced through it, at first not comprehending what it was. She went back and slowly read the first couple of pages, carefully digesting every word. Then the full impact of the document hit her.

She glared at the attorney, a touch of anger

surrounding her words. "This is a prenuptial agreement stating that I relinquish any and all claim to Chance's assets, and it extends to cover the Fowler family assets and Fowler Industries."

"That's correct, Miss Roper. If you would just sign here—" he indicated the exact spot for her signature "—and also here."

She stared at the attorney in disbelief. He stood there as if he expected her to zip through the numerous pages of legalese, then sign it while he waited. She did not know which had hit her first, the anger or the hurt. She made a valiant attempt to keep her anger under control and the hurt out of her voice. She shoved the file folder back toward the attorney, but kept one copy of the document clutched tightly in her hand.

She spoke from between clenched teeth. "I have no intention of signing any such document and you can tell Mr. Chance Fowler that I find his attitude appalling." She gulped in a steadying breath but it did not take the sharp edge from her words. "And in light of the fact that the subject of marriage has never even been broached, I am deeply offended by his actions."

When the attorney made no effort to leave, she reinforced her position. *"Goodbye,* Mr. Dunlop."

Marcie buried any and all emotion and did not move a muscle as she watched him calmly return the file folder in his attaché case.

"I'll be in touch, Miss Roper." With that he snapped the lid shut, picked up the case, turned and left the building.

On the outside she maintained a composed demeanor, but inside only her anger kept her from crumbling under the weight of the horrible pain that stabbed at her consciousness. The anger and the pain churned together as she tried to separate the feelings. She felt as if she had been kicked in the stomach. She could not even begin to imagine what had prompted Chance to have such a document drawn up. And to have his attorney present it to her in such a cold, callous manner, as if she were nothing more than a business matter to be dealt with, was beyond her comprehension.

She could not believe the unmitigated arrogance of Chance Fowler. Apparently he had just assumed that she was dying to marry him and all he could think of was protecting his precious money from her greedy clutches. The anger took hold, along with a newly mounted sense of determination. She would make sure he fully understood that the world did not revolve around his wishes. She had gotten along very nicely before he had invaded her life and she would continue to get along just fine without him.

The pain edged out the anger as the truth settled over her. She knew she could not lie to herself. It would be a devastating blow to her if Chance ceased to be part of her life. She shook her head in dismay. She simply did not know what to make of the attorney's visit and the document he had wanted her to sign. Maybe it would have made a little bit of sense if she and Chance had actually talked about the future or even the exact nature of their relationship, but it was a conversation that had never happened. Chance had made his beliefs very clear where commitment was concerned and she had never challenged them.

The anger finally managed to gain the upper hand once again, spurring her into action. She snatched the phone receiver from its cradle and dialed Chance's number. The phone rang twice, then his answering machine picked up the call. She hung up the phone. It would serve no purpose to vent her anger at an answering machine. She needed to handle this in a mature, adult manner...and in person.

She took a calming breath. "I am in control. I am in control." Saying it out loud did not help. She felt about as in control as a toothpick in a tornado. She desperately needed to sort out her feelings, to separate the anger from the hurt and the confusion from the despair so she could handle this in a mature and rational manner.

She stared at the document. She would not have believed that Chance could do such a thing to her, but here it was, staring her in the face. A prenuptial agreement. She never would have believed that the man she loved could be so cold and calculating. The logical side of her said to remain calm, that she had not heard Chance's explanation for the document, that she was reacting in an irrational manner.

But try as she might, she could not shake the hurt and the anger.

Marcie stuck her head out the back door and called to Glen. "I've had something come up and I need to go home. Would you close up for me tonight?"

"No problem, Marcie." He looked at her

quizzically. "Is there something wrong? Anything I can help with?"

"No...nothing's wrong." She heard the catch in her voice as she started to speak. She hoped Glen would not notice it. "Just some unexpected news...a problem I need to take care of, that's all."

"Are you sure?"

She extended a confident smile. "I'm sure."

"Okay. I'll see you in the morning."

She grabbed the distasteful document, shoved it in her purse, and hurried out the front door. She drove straight home, her mind reeling in a mass of confusion as she fought back the tears of despair.

"Come on, get that piece of junk off the road!" The irritation raced through Chance, assaulting every corner of his existence as he drove toward Crestview Bay. Why did every bad driver in the state find it necessary to poke along in front of him? It took all his self-control to keep from floorboarding the accelerator and charging around the offending car and driver.

The fact that she had taken off work early because of an emergency was cause enough for concern, but Glen's comment that something was wrong and that Marcie had seemed upset had him more than merely concerned. And then when she did not answer her phone after Glen specifically said she had told him she was going home…well, there was nothing to do other than get to her house as quickly as possible.

He screeched to a halt in her driveway, hurtled up the front steps, and banged loudly on the front door. ''Marcie, open up! Are you in there? Marcie?''

The sound of someone pounding on her door startled Marcie out of her self-inflicted misery. She had been curled up in the large easy chair trying to figure out exactly when everything had gone wrong. She had always known that there was a distinct possibility that the differences in their backgrounds would end up coming between them, but she had never imagined that it would happen this way. Having an attorney draw up a prenuptial agreement and hand deliver it to her for a signature was not something that would have just occurred to him that morning. It had to have been on his mind for a while, something that he had previously authorized.

Then she heard Chance's voice. He must have gotten word from his attorney that she had refused to sign the document and had come to confront her in person about it. Well, that suited her just fine. They needed to have it out here and now. She felt her determination slip a little as she heaved a sigh of resignation at the inevitable and rose to her feet.

As soon as she opened the door, Chance rushed inside, grabbed her and pulled her into his arms. The concern in his voice came through loud and clear...and confused her.

"Are you okay? What's wrong?"

Marcie squirmed out of his embrace and took a couple of steps away from him. This certainly was not what she had anticipated.

"I'm fine...considering." Her words were clipped in spite of her attempt to project a neutral manner. She wanted more than anything to be able to handle things in a mature and intelligent manner and not let her emotions take control. There was no need to make a scene, no need to turn this into an unpleasant situation. She had always known that Chance would never make a commitment to a relationship. Things between them were obviously over and she would simply have to learn to live with it...although she did not have the slightest notion of how.

Chance's brow furrowed in confusion. "I don't understand. What do you mean by 'considering'? What's wrong?"

She stiffened to attention. How dare he ask her such a stupid question. "You should certainly know."

A flash of irritation darted through him and clung to his words. "Don't do that to me, Marcie. Don't hand me that old if-you-don't-know-then-I'm-not-going-to-tell-you line of garbage. I think you owe me more consideration than that. It should be obvious that if I knew what was wrong I wouldn't be standing here asking you. I called you at work and Glen said you'd gone home and seemed very upset about something. I called and when you didn't answer I became worried, so here I am."

He eyed her suspiciously. "You're obviously all right physically, so what's going on here?"

So that was his game. He was going to pretend that he did not know what had happened. Well, she could pretend the same thing, too. "Very well...if that's how you want to handle it."

She retrieved her purse and removed the document. "Here." She thrust it into his hands. "Your attorney gave this to me a few hours ago and wanted me to sign it. Are you trying to tell me you don't know anything about it? That all by himself your attorney decided it would be fun to draw up this document and ask me to sign it for no apparent reason?"

"My attorney?" He glanced at the document she had shoved at him, his face covered in bewilderment.

"I can't believe how wrong I was about you." A sob caught in her throat. She tried to swallow it. "It pains me to realize that you're nothing more than that arrogant playboy who grabbed me on the street what now seems like so long ago. Do you feel that every woman in the world is simply dying to have you give her a second look?"

She turned away from him, preferring to stare out the front window. She did not want him to see the mist forming in her eyes as the pain settled in her heart. "I know your feelings on the subject of relationships and commitment. You've made them perfectly clear. But I still thought we had something very special in spite of that, something very real even if unspoken. I had resigned myself to the fact that you'd never make a commitment to the future and I thought I could live with that reality.''

She took a steadying breath in an attempt to shove down the emotion that welled inside her. The very last thing she wanted to do was cry. She would not give him the satisfaction of seeing her tears and knowing the depth of her despair.

She continued to stare out the window. ''So I can't help but wonder just why, in light of the fact that I had never asked you for a commitment or discussed the future for our relationship, you found it necessary to present me with a prenuptial agreement to sign since marriage had never even been hinted at, let alone mentioned.''

When she did not hear any response she turned around to face him. What she saw was certainly not what she had expected. Total bewilderment blanketed his features as he stared at the document. It was almost as if he had not heard a word she had said. He finally looked up at her, total confusion surrounding his words.

''This is a prenuptial agreement. Where did it come from?''

"Weren't you listening to me?" An edge of irritation crept into her voice. "Your attorney brought it to me this afternoon and wanted me to sign it."

"My attorney? Kevin Prichard came to see you and brought you this to sign? Where did he get it?"

"Kevin Prichard? Who's Kevin Prichard?" Now she was as confused as he seemed to be.

"He's my attorney. And I certainly don't have any idea why he would come to see you. And as for this..." He held up the document. "I haven't a clue what this is about."

"No, that wasn't the name of the man who came to see me. His name was George Dun—"

Chance's eyes widened in shock. "George Dunlop?" Intense anger contorted his features as he spit out the words. "He's my *father's* attorney." His voice dropped to a mere whisper, his words almost inaudible. "So that's it...dear ol' Dad's fine hand."

"Your father?" She took a couple of steps closer to him. "I don't understand. Why would your father do this? It doesn't make any sense. You and I...we've never even discussed the future...uh, I mean what the future held.

We've never talked about a relationship...or commitment or, uh..."

Her words trailed off. She did not know exactly what to say or think. Just a minute ago she was hurt and angry. She knew she would never see Chance again, that her heart and soul had been ripped from her reality. She also knew she had been mad enough to have punched him. But now she didn't know what to think or feel. She did know that the series of emotions that had crossed Chance's face—the shock followed by the confusion and finally the anger—had been genuine.

She felt everything drain from her body, everything except her bewilderment over what had just happened. What in the world would be next? She did not have to wait long for an answer.

Chance pulled her into his arms. Her body trembled in his embrace. He stroked her hair while cradling her head against his shoulder. She was not the only one experiencing a very real physical reaction to a highly emotional predicament. He had to make things right. He had to make her understand, to believe him that he had nothing to do with this.

His words came out soft and caring. "I'm

so sorry about this, Marcie. Please believe that I didn't know anything about it. I would never do anything like this to you. This is just the type of thing my father would have done. It's apparently his response to my having brought you to his house for Christmas dinner with the family. True to his philosophy of life, his first and foremost thought was to protect his material possessions. And having been married six times now, he's certainly an expert on prenuptial agreements."

She sought out the truth in his eyes. She knew she looked as perplexed as she felt. "But why would he assume that we're, uh…"

"That we're getting married?"

She glanced shyly at the floor as the embarrassment overcame her. "Uh, yes…getting married."

For the first time the idea of marriage solidified in his mind. He knew the thought had tried to present itself before and he had always managed to shove it away. He was not exactly sure what to say or how to say it, but he had to say something.

He tried to force a casual tone to his voice, anything to cover the anxiety that pulled at him. "Well, maybe for once dear ol' Dad is right. Maybe we should just go ahead and get married." A nervous chuckle escaped his throat. "What do you think?"

It was as if someone had just dumped a bucket of ice water over her head. The instant shock knocked her into reality faster than she thought possible. She backed out of his arms, then quickly put a couple of additional steps between them. She did not like the quaver she heard in her voice, but she could not force any control to it. It took all the strength she could muster to force out the words. She could not stop the single tear than ran down her cheek. "I think that's the lousiest, most insensitive thing I've ever heard."

He stared at her in stunned silence for a moment. "You what?"

"You make it sound as if it's no more significant than deciding which movie to go see, and if that's your attitude toward our *relationship,* or whatever it is that we have, then I don't want any part of it." Those had been the most difficult words she had ever spoken, and what she was about to say would be even more difficult. But she knew she had to say it before she lost her nerve.

When he did not immediately respond, she

walked toward the front door. "There doesn't seem to be anything left to say so...I—I think you'd better leave now."

Chance reached out for her, but she stepped aside to avoid his touch. Her words were surrounded by determination, although her insides churned in turmoil. "Please don't make this any more difficult for me than it already is."

"Why are you doing this, Marcie? Please don't let my father drive this wedge between us."

"The problem is not your father. Everything was so marvelous and I was so happy that I had almost convinced myself I could handle your not being able to make a commitment. Well, I can't. You obviously don't take us or our relationship seriously. I can't accept a half-hearted flippant we-might-as-well type of proposal, one that doesn't even mention the word love."

The tears welled to the brims of her eyes and a sob caught in her throat. "I also can't expect you to stick by a commitment that didn't come willingly. You could never be happy with the type of stable home life that is so important to me. You would feel tied down. I can see that now. I tried to close my eyes to it, but you forced them wide open. We simply want different things out of life.''

She tried desperately to blink away the tears and maintain control of her emotions. ''I hope you find whatever it is that will make you happy and fulfill your life.''

Panic filled his voice and echoed through his words. ''What are you talking about? I already know what I need...who I need.''

''Goodbye, Chance.'' She quickly edged him out the front door in spite of his protests and closed it before he could say or do anything more. The last thing she wanted at that moment was to hear him say he loved her, whether he meant it or not. Her heart was breaking, but she knew she had done the right thing. In time she would get over Chance Fowler. Meanwhile life would go on.

She glanced around the living room, at the decorations they had put up together, at the strands of popcorn and cranberries they had draped over the branches of the Christmas tree. And at the package with Chance's name on it that she had carefully wrapped and placed under the tree. What she had thought would be the best Christmas ever was now going to be the worst...and the loneliest.

* * *

Chance stared at Marcie's front door, the one she had closed at the same time as she had symbolically closed him out of her life. He went back to his car and sat in it for a few minutes while trying to get his thoughts and feelings together. He seemed to be split in two directions. One direction said he should go back to the door and kick it in if necessary and force her to sit down and listen to him. He quickly ruled that out. He knew he could not force her to listen.

That left only one viable direction. He needed to figure out what he could do to make things right with her again. He stared at the legal document he still clutched in his hand. The anger seethed inside him. The first step in that direction was to deal with his father before he did anything else.

All his thoughts were overshadowed by the panic that asked what he would do if Marcie refused to be part of his life again. He knew he had blown it big time. As soon as the maybe we-should-just-go-ahead-and-get-married words were out of his mouth he knew it was the worst thing he could have said. He also knew at that moment that the one thing he wanted above all else was to be married to Marcie, for them to make a home together and raise a family.

But first things first.

Chance drove directly to his father's house, barged into the study over the objections of the butler, and threw the crumpled document on the desk in front of a startled Douglas Fowler.

Chance snapped out his words through barely controlled anger. "Do you want to explain to me what the hell you had in mind when you sent George Dunlop to see Marcie with this piece of crap in his hand?"

Douglas Fowler reached for his cigar humidor, obviously stalling for time while collecting his thoughts. Chance was in no mood to put up with him or his annoying tactics. He brushed the humidor aside.

"I want an answer and I want it right now!" His demand was met with silence.

"Okay. If you don't want to tell me what you were attempting to do, then let me tell you what you've accomplished." Chance noted the way his father's gaze darted uneasily around the room, as if searching for a way out of an unpleasant situation.

"I was content to allow my relationship

with Marcie Roper to continue just the way it had been—no commitment, no talk of the future. But when she confronted me with this stupid document, called me an arrogant jerk, and threw me out of her house, it really opened my eyes. Thanks to your meddling, I now have the courage to do what I should have done a long time ago.''

''Think about what you're doing, Chance. Love is a fleeting thing. What is bliss now can be hell a year from now. And then where will you be? You'll be stuck with an expensive financial settlement, giving away your money to some little gold digger who isn't worth it.''

Chance allowed a sneer of contempt. ''Well, I know you speak from experience on that one.''

''Then why do you continually go out of your way to ignore my experience and advice?''

''That's your life, but it's not mine. I've found a wonderful woman and I want to spend the rest of my life with her. I realize that's a foreign concept to you, but I now know how right it is for me.''

Chance turned and left his father's house.

First step down and one step yet to go.

He had tomorrow, Wednesday and most of Thursday to accomplish everything he needed to do by Christmas Eve. There could be no slip-ups, no mistakes. Everything had to be perfect. His entire future was at stake.

His head was filled with so many thoughts as he drove home. A wife, a home, a family—things that had never mattered to him before were now more important to him than anything else in the world. He refused to allow a conflicting thought or even a hint that things might not go exactly as he wanted. He and Marcie would be married and they would live happily ever after and that was all there was to it.

Marcie locked the doors of the nursery at noon on Thursday. She always gave her employees half a day off on December 24 in addition to Christmas Day. All around her everyone bustled with excitement—holiday festivities, friends getting together, and family celebrations. Glen's parents had come all the way from Michigan to spend Christmas with him. It was a time of love and closeness.

But not for Marcie Roper. Several people had extended invitations for her to join them and their families for Christmas Eve and

Christmas Day. She had thanked them, but had declined the offers. She put up a cheery front, assuring everyone that she had plans and would not be spending the holiday alone.

No sooner had she arrived home than the loneliness began to close in around her. She had not seen Chance nor even heard from him since she had shoved him out her front door Monday evening. It had been her decision and she had been adamant about it. She had also been miserable.

She turned on television. *It's a Wonderful Life* with Jimmy Stewart. She changed channels. *Miracle on 34th Street.* Someone else's happily-ever-after was not what she wanted to see. She changed channels again. The Weather Channel. That would be perfect. She could see what miserable weather other parts of the country were having compared to the warm sunshine of San Diego. Maybe that would cheer her up a little bit.

She settled into the corner of the couch and stared at the television. The emotional strain of the past couple of days quickly took its toll. Her eyelids grew heavy and in a couple of minutes she had dozed off. It was more of an unconscious effort to blot out everything bad than it was a need for sleep.

She wasn't sure if she had just fallen asleep or if she had been sleeping for a while when the insistent buzzing of the doorbell woke her. She shook the grogginess from her head as she rose from the couch. Who could be ringing the bell on Christmas Eve? She certainly was not expecting anyone.

She opened the door and found herself staring into the handsome features of Chance Fowler. Before she could say anything, he stepped inside and shoved the door closed with his foot. He carried a large box, which he deposited on the floor, then he escorted her to the couch. She started to speak, but he stilled her words.

"Before you say anything, I want you to sit there and hear me out. Okay?" He touched his finger to her lips. "Just nod your head."

She did not know what was happening, but she nodded her head in agreement.

He opened the large box, brought out a bouquet of one dozen long-stemmed roses, and handed them to her. "These are for you— beautiful roses for a beautiful lady."

She inhaled the fragrance, then looked up at

him. Their gazes locked for an intimate moment. She did not understand what was happening, or why he was there.

He reached into the box again and withdrew a bottle of chilled champagne and two glasses. He opened the bottle, filled the two glasses, and handed one of them to her.

"I would like to propose a toast." He held his glass out toward her. She hesitated a moment then lifted her glass. "Here's to a very memorable night and a Merry Christmas...the first of many." He clinked his glass against hers, then took a sip.

"Flowers and champagne?" There was a reticence to her voice that showed her skepticism and questioned his intentions. "I don't understand what's going on here, Chance."

"Don't say anything yet. There's one more item." He nervously shifted his weight from one foot to the other. His voice contained less confidence than it had just seconds earlier.

"I, uh, I've never done this before and I'm not sure exactly how to go about it." He cleared his throat as he glanced down at the floor. He swallowed his anxiety, then took a calming breath before once again focusing on her beautiful face. He reached into his pocket and withdrew a small velvet box. Then in a spontaneous gesture, he dropped to one knee.

"Marcie..." He reached out and took her hand in his. "Marcie...I love you very much. I've never said that to another woman. You are the first and the only woman I have ever loved or ever will love." He opened the box and took out the diamond ring. "Would you do me the honor of marrying me? I want us to spend the rest of our lives together and the only legal document I'm interested in is a marriage license." The apprehension churned in the pit of his stomach as he waited for her to say something.

She stared at the diamond ring he held in his hand. Never in her wildest imaginings or flights of fantasy had she ever envisioned this scene—Chance Fowler down on one knee, asking her to marry him. Her voice was soft, her words almost a whisper. "I—I don't know what to say."

"Why don't you just say yes?" He tried to extend a confident smile, but it showed more apprehension than anything else.

Marcie's words were hesitant. "I have some concerns..." She had more than mere concerns. She was scared.

"Concerns?" This was definitely not what he wanted to hear.

She reached out and lightly touched her fingertips against his cheek. He grasped her hand in his and held it against his chest. She felt his heartbeat at the same time as she felt at one with him. But she still had concerns.

"I love you, Chance. I love you so much it hurts. Sometimes I wonder if I love you too much."

She loved him. The words burned into his consciousness. The pure ecstasy of the moment welled inside him until there was no room for anything else. But it only lasted for a moment. Then the rest of what she had said seeped into his consciousness. This was not going the way he thought it would...not at all. "How is it possible to love someone too much?"

"I'm scared, Chance. This scares me."

He sat next to her on the couch, putting his arm around her shoulder and pulling her body close to his. "I'm a little scared, too. I've never asked anyone to marry me before. It's a big step. But you love me and I certainly love you. What more do we need than that?"

"You say that now, and I'm sure you truly mean it. But..."

"But what?" He placed his fingertips under her chin and lifted her face so that he could look into her eyes. "What's bothering you, Marcie? Is it that you don't want to get married? Am I rushing you? I know we haven't known each other that long, less than two months, but I've never been so sure of anything in my entire life."

"Are you really sure? What happens months from now when you begin to wonder if you were coerced into asking me to marry you? Or even years from now, when you decide you need more excitement in your life than marriage provides?"

He leaned his face into hers and brushed a soft kiss against her lips. "You're talking foolishness. I'm asking you to marry me because I love you and want very much for us to be a family. You, Marcie Roper, are all the excitement I need or want in my life. Please say you'll marry me." He literally held his breath as he waited for her to respond.

"I can't imagine life without you, Chance..."

There was a hesitancy to her words that sent

a shiver of trepidation through his body. "Is that a yes?"

She closed her eyes for a moment and held her breath as she gathered her composure. "Are you sure, Chance? Are you really sure this is what you want?"

"I've never been more sure of anything in my life."

She leaned her face into his and placed a loving kiss on his lips. "Then I would be honored to be Mrs. Chance Fowler."

The smile spread across his face as he slipped the diamond ring on her finger. "Merry Christmas, Marcie. My Christmas wish has come true. You've just made me the happiest man in the world."

He pulled her into his embrace and held her tightly as she rested her head against his shoulder. And the room filled with a love that would last a lifetime.

* * * * *

SILHOUETTE®

LARGE PRINT TITLES FOR
JULY – DECEMBER 2001

SPECIAL EDITION®

July:	OLDER, WISER...PREGNANT	Marilyn Pappano
August:	THE WINNING HAND	Nora Roberts
September:	HEART OF THE HUNTER	Lindsay McKenna
October:	FATHER-TO-BE	Laurie Paige
November:	THE MILLIONAIRE BACHELOR	Susan Mallery
December:	THE PRESIDENT'S DAUGHTER	Annette Broadrick

DESIRE®

July:	BELOVED	Diana Palmer
August:	THE NON-COMMISSIONED BABY	Maureen Child
September:	LOVE ME TRUE	Ann Major
October:	THE OLDEST LIVING MARRIED VIRGIN	Maureen Child
November:	CALLAGHAN'S BRIDE	Diana Palmer
December:	THE MILLIONAIRE'S CHRISTMAS WISH	Shawna Delacorte

SENSATION®

July:	IF A MAN ANSWERS	Merline Lovelace
August:	A MAN LIKE MORGAN KANE	Beverly Barton
September:	EVERYDAY, AVERAGE JONES	Suzanne Brockmann
October:	ROYAL'S CHILD	Sharon Sala
November:	ENGAGING SAM	Ingrid Weaver
December:	GABRIEL HAWK'S LADY	Beverly Barton